Sea
of
Love

HARPER BLISS

Also by Harper Bliss

Release the Stars
Once in a Lifetime
At the Water's Edge
French Kissing Season Two
French Kissing Season One
High Rise (The Complete Collection)

Copyright © 2016 Harper Bliss
Cover picture © Depositphotos / AnnaOmelchenko / paprika_
Cover design by Caroline Manchoulas
Published by Ladylit Publishing – a division of Q.P.S. Projects Limited -
Hong Kong

ISBN-13 978-988-14205-7-2

For my wife, who supports and loves me through all the seasons.

CHAPTER ONE

I try to recline my seat, but as soon as I push the button and apply some pressure, I feel the knees of the passenger behind me resisting my attempt. Perhaps I should have listened to Miranda when she told me to book a business class ticket. "But this is not a business trip," I'd said, to which she'd just responded with a sigh. Not that I would ever buy an overpriced ticket just to have some more room on *any* trip—or that I ever go on business trips.

"Some more wine, Ma'am?" a female member of the cabin crew asks.

"No, thank you." I hand her my empty plastic cup. I've had two units already. Despite this being the start of a long overdue holiday, I won't let go of my health principles so easily.

I close my eyes, the back of my seat straight again, and think about the two weeks of absolute nothingness stretching out in front of me.

"At the end of your life, you won't wish you had worked more, Alice," Miranda said a few months ago. "As your partner in this company, I demand you take three weeks off this summer." She'd offered me her phone and had me flick through some pictures of blue skies and a stylish house a few minutes from the beach in Quinta do Lago. "Consider it booked. How does August 1st till August 21st sound?"

"Three weeks? Have you lost your mind?" I'd glared at her, but had difficulty keeping my gaze off her phone. The last picture she'd shown me was of the swimming pool, which was bathed in the most exquisite light, the water a reflection of all things summer. It didn't help that she came to me with this on one of London's more dreary days. "Fine, but it'll have to be two weeks. Three is just ludicrous."

Miranda had stretched out her hand and demanded we'd shake on the deal. Apart from a day here and there and a long weekend in Paris or down the coast in Cornwall, I'm not much of a holidaymaker. I'd rather work than spend too much time with my own thoughts, a work ethic that, in my humble opinion, has allowed Miranda to earn enough money to actually buy that house in the Algarve.

But Miranda got her wish and here I am. The plane is about to land at Faro airport.

After going through all airport shenanigans—another reason to only ever travel by car or train—I pick up my rental car and spread out the map over the steering wheel. The lady behind the counter said the car came with a sat nav, but I like to find my destination the old-fashioned way.

By the time I arrive at Miranda's house, I'm more than ready for a dip in that pool. And I have to agree with her, because as I park my car in front of the house, a sense of summer, of intense leisure, comes over me. A sensation I've never experienced anywhere else. Not for a long while, anyway. I'm tired from the journey, but just arriving here engulfs me in an aura of relaxation.

The house looks every bit as stunning as in the pictures. It's not overly big, but its white walls look picturesque against the blue of the sky, and the pool is surrounded by grass so green and lush, that someone must water it on a daily basis. I hope they won't intrude on the complete privacy Miranda guaranteed me for the two weeks I'm taking up residence here.

I only brought one suitcase, and I wheel it into the master bedroom, which looks out over the pool area. I inhale deeply, and let the stress of London, work, and the journey here wash off me a little with every exhale.

Before I relax completely and enjoy the rest of this

beautiful day, I should get some exercise. The flight was only three hours, but the entire journey took about seven, and my legs are stiff from sitting down too much. In London, my favourite—and only—means of exercise is an hour every morning before work on the stair walker I set up in my spare bedroom. It's a great way to catch up on the news and stay in shape. When I asked Miranda if there was any gym equipment in her house she'd looked at me funnily, as though that was the most outrageous question ever, even though most hotels around the globe boast some sort of gym on their premises.

"Just relax," Miranda had said. "Two weeks off won't destroy your excellent physical condition, Alice."

It's not a hardship to have to make do with the pool. I'm not the world's best swimmer, but it will be good for my biceps, triceps, and deltoids, not to mention release the tension from my legs. I can be adaptable, I want to say to Miranda, but I'll have to save it for when I see her again in two weeks.

After I've emptied my suitcase and given my clothes their rightful place in the wardrobe, I slip into my one-piece bathing suit. I also splashed out on a bikini with a loud floral print and, looking at it again, wonder what on earth came over me when I purchased it. A one-piece will do.

The water is not warm, but not cold either. It's just the right temperature and before launching into a few laps for sporty reasons, I float on my back, the late afternoon sun still strong enough to pierce underneath my eyelids.

The pool isn't very long, so I count my laps until I've reached forty, after which I sit on the ledge panting. A tall tree casts my chosen spot in shadows, and I breathe in to acquaint myself with the summery smells surrounding me. When Miranda first told me she was buying a house here, I accused her of being foolish with money, but sitting here now, I guess I'm beginning to understand. She's had this place for eighteen years, has asked me to come here a thousand times, and I see now that I was the foolish one for always having a good reason not to. But summers here were booked up with Miranda and her daughter spending at least a month in the house—a luxury I often scolded her for—and, after Alan left me, I was working all the time anyway. What was I going to do coming here on my own? And travelling with Miranda and her daughter somehow never appealed to me. I don't dislike children, but, for relaxation purposes, I would never deliberately seek out their company either.

When my stomach starts growling, I take a shower and head into the nearest village. I buy enough food to last me a few days and two bottles of wine.

Just when I arrive back at the villa, my phone rings. Miranda advised me to turn it off and hide it in a cupboard, but that was simply one stretch too far. When I look at the screen, I see it's Miranda calling. Maybe to check if I would answer. Of course I do.

"Alice, isn't it glorious? Listen to this." She does something with the phone and I hear a buzzing noise. "That's the sound of a lovely London rain storm pelting against my office window."

"It's rather amazing." I lean against the table in the open-plan kitchen and I can see the swimming pool from here as well.

"How do you feel?"

How do I feel? Miranda learnt to not ask me that question a long time ago. "Erm, great." The irony is perfectly audible in my voice.

"Are you relaxed?" She pauses. "Because, well, um, there's something…" It's not Miranda's style to do this much hemming and hawing.

"Is it Mr. Pappas? I knew I shouldn't—"

"No, Alice, relax. It's got nothing to do with work." She clears her throat. "It's Joy. She's unexpectedly starting a new job in a week and she'd like to enjoy a bit of summer before going back to work."

"Okay. Then she should." I fail to understand why this upsets Miranda so much. She should be happy Joy has a new job, the way that girl flutters from employer to employer.

"Yes, well, the thing is, Alice, she's asked if she could go to the house… just for a few days. Just for some much needed vitamin D."

Is Miranda talking about *this* house? She can't be. I'm here. I was promised privacy and solitude. "Joy wants to come *here?*" For once, I don't hide the outright indignation in my voice.

"Only if you agree. I mean, the house is more than big enough for the two of you. She won't be a nuisance, I promise you that. She'll be at the beach most of the time, anyway. You'll barely notice she's there."

No, a little voice in my head screams. But this is Miranda's house. What am I supposed to say? Your own flesh and blood can't use it because I'm here? It goes against every rule of politeness I've ever lived by. "Well," I start, but Miranda cuts me off again.

"It'll only be for a few days. She needs to come back and start work."

I roll my eyes. The lows Miranda stoops to for her daughter, while a simple "No, the house is occupied" would have sufficed. I don't know Joy very well. I haven't seen her in years, but I guess Miranda hasn't stopped spoiling her after she graduated from university.

"It's fine, Miranda. I'll welcome her with open arms." *But only because you're not giving me a choice.* Miranda knew full well I wouldn't say no. It's probably much easier for her to make this phone call to me than to say no to her daughter. Children. Neither Alan nor I were very interested in pursuing a traditional family. I got all the satisfaction I needed from pouring all my energy into my career.

"Thank you so much. I owe you," Miranda says. "I'm well aware. I'll make it up to you somehow, I swear."

Miranda then proceeds to tell me Joy, who is apparently sitting next to her while she makes the call to Portugal, will book her flight straightaway. She'll be there tomorrow afternoon. No need to pick her up at the airport, she'll get her own car. A rental Miranda will pay for, I'm sure. By the time I put down the phone, my relaxed state has all but dissipated. So much for my holiday. While I prepare a simple salad, I think of ways to make Miranda pay for this. She's the one who was so dead set on me going on holiday in the first place. It just goes to show where her loyalties lie. Blood is always thicker than the waters of friendship, even though we've been friends since before Joy was born.

While I eat my salad overlooking the pool, I exceed my self-imposed daily alcohol limit by drinking two more glasses of wine.

CHAPTER TWO

Joy arrives in a bright yellow Mini Cooper—a vehicle I didn't even know car rental agencies provided—with just a backpack as luggage.

"You travel light," is the first thing I say to her, which isn't very courteous, but I can't help it. I feel as though I need to make clear from the start that I don't fully agree with how my holiday is being rudely interrupted.

"No need for a lot of clothes here." Joy shoulders her backpack and walks briskly towards me. "Good to see you, Alice. It's been ages." She opens her arms wide. Is she really expecting a hug? I can't even remember the last time I embraced someone. Before I even have a chance to think of an acceptable manner to refuse her hug, she's thrown her arms around me and pulls me close to her. I find this manner of greeting a mere acquaintance highly impertinent, and squirm my way out of her impromptu cuddle quickly. When I take a step back she looks at me funnily. "Good grief, Alice, do you have a funeral to attend or something?"

I did throw on black trousers as Joy's arrival time approached, and covered my upper body with a cream silk blouse. "Some of us like to dress properly," I retort, and let my glance roam over Joy's scantily clad body. She's wearing a tank top through which I can clearly see the contours of a black bra and a pair of shorts that barely covers her behind.

She shrugs and heads into the house, dropping her backpack on the kitchen floor. "Mum has given me instructions to not bother you and avoid you as much as possible." She opens the fridge door and peers inside. "I promise I'll go grocery shopping tomorrow, but the food on the plane was horrible and I'm starving." She turns to me, the fridge door still open. "And gagging for a dip in that pool." She steps a little farther into the coolness of the wide-open fridge door. "Oh gosh, that feels good."

Have you lost your mind? I want to ask. Has your mother not taught you how to save energy and behave responsibly? But I've never been very adept at communicating my inner emotions—and I never had much need to. "Take whatever you want," I say, instead. "I'll be in my room."

"Thanks," Joy shouts after me. Already, the effects of the one day of unwinding I got to enjoy are undone. A tightness has crept back into my muscles, and my brain is going into overdrive coming up with ways to make the best of this situation. I lie on my bed, the French windows opened to the pool area, and leaf through a Lee Child book absentmindedly, producing no results. The next five days with Joy will simply be one of those occurrences in life I'll have to suffer through. Silently, of course, because that's what I do.

I hear stumbling in the adjoining room. There's another bedroom on the other side of the house, but it doesn't lead directly to the pool area. I do hope Joy will at least have good enough manners to not make too much noise during the night. A little later, I see two legs appear in my field of vision. They're supple, their skin unblemished by age, and they patter to the pool. When I let my glance drift upwards, along a piece of fabric that can hardly be called a pair of bikini bottoms, I can't believe what I see: Joy's back is bare. There's no sign of any string across her back. All I see is naked flesh. I don't have time to ponder this further, because with a neat splash, Joy dives into the pool.

Shocked, I sit up. Is this how she intends not to bother me? The nerve of this girl. I have to stop myself from reaching for my phone and calling Miranda. But all of this is

Miranda's fault in the first place, and what is she going to do? Call her daughter and tell her to put on a top? That's even more unlikely than me joining Joy in the pool when she's dressed like that.

My eyes are still trained on the surface of the pool. Not because I want to see, but because I haven't been able to look away, so stupefied am I with Joy's choice of non-dress. All of a sudden, her head bursts through the surface of the water, her face slick and her hair wet, and she rests her arms on the edge.

"Are you going to take those funeral clothes off today or what?" She plasters a self-satisfied grin on her face.

So much for my privacy. Perhaps *I* should move to the room at the back of the house, so she can't look into my bedroom every time she goes for a swim. I'm still too stunned to speak. Thank goodness her arms are just resting on the edge, and her nude torso is hidden from my view.

"The water is gorgeous." Joy tips her head to the side. "Or are you going to sulk in your room all evening?"

Who does this girl think she is? To talk to me this way? Clearly, Miranda hasn't taught her about respecting her elders either.

Joy proceeds to hoist herself up out of the pool and sit down cross-legged in the grass, facing me with her bare breasts on full display. To my great dismay, I feel my cheeks flush. I can only hope the distance between my bed and the pool is big enough so Joy doesn't notice.

"I shall continue to read my book." I'm happy with the ounce of dignity I manage to inject into my voice.

"Oh yeah? What are you reading?" Joy just doesn't leave me alone. She's probably been showered with so much attention throughout her life that she can't be on her own for five minutes.

"Just the new Jack Reacher." I picked it up at the WHSmith at the airport. I don't often allow myself guilty pleasures like these. But, if anything, it seems like the sort of book Joy would like.

"That crap. Really?" She squints. "I hadn't pegged you for the type, Alice. You surprise me."

"Oh, and I presume your library is only filled with the likes of Ian McEwan and Margaret Atwood?" I retort before I even give myself a chance to think.

"My library?" Joy chuckles. "If you mean the one on my Kindle, then, I guess, yes, my preferences in literature are pretty high-brow." With drops of water slipping down her cheeks like that, and her long blond hair a tight, wet cap on her head, she looks like the least high-brow person I've ever seen. She probably attends raves and watches reality television—the greatest waste of time ever invented.

It's hard to have this conversation while drops of water trickle down Joy's neck, slide down her breasts and pool in between her crossed legs. "Good for you," is all I say, not wanting to extend this awkward moment.

Joy cocks her head, squints her eyes.

"What?" I can't help but ask.

"I was just trying to remember how long it's been since I saw you last and if you were already so uptight back then."

Uptight? I clap the book I'm holding shut and throw it onto the nightstand. "I didn't come all the way to Portugal to get judged by a teenager." I jump off the bed and start closing the windows.

"I'm twenty-nine years old, Alice," Joy half-yells. "Haven't been a teenager in a very long time."

Without acknowledging what she says further, I shut the windows on her, erasing this brazen girl from my field of vision—as though it can somehow magically make her disappear from the property. I stand by the window long enough to hear Joy splash into the pool again. The sound of carelessness, I think, of a recklessness I've never known.

I switch on the air-conditioning in the room because, immediately, it's too hot and stuffy with the windows closed, and I welcome the gentle whir that drowns out the slapping noises Joy makes outside.

The blouse clings to the small of my back in the humidity—perhaps she had a point there. While I slip out of my formal clothes, I contemplate changing my flight, because this holiday will leave me more stressed than when I first arrived. In the end, it's stubbornness that makes me stay. I can wait Joy out. She'll only be here for a few days and after she's left, the sense of relief and long-awaited solitude will bring me an altogether new kind of peace of mind.

CHAPTER THREE

A couple of hours later, I venture out of my room and onto the patio for a snack. I refuse to confine myself to the kitchen just because Joy is sleeping topless in a lounger on the other side of the pool. I wouldn't normally get out the wine at this time of day, but my nerves are frayed, and seeing as I'm trapped in the house with Joy, it seems like the only way to relax myself a tiny bit. As I dip bread into olive oil, my eyes wander. Not even in my twenties would I ever have considered taking off my bikini top. Not under any circumstance. But I'm well aware that, across generations, things change. I have twenty-two years on Joy, and she might as well have descended upon Quinta do Lago from another planet. When I was twenty-nine, I had been married to Alan for four years—and he'd barely seen my breasts before we said "I do".

"I'll have a glass of that," Joy suddenly says, her eyes only half-open.

Does she expect me to serve her now as well? "Be my guest." I take my glass of wine and take a few gulps, hoping that my gaze wasn't trained on her chest when she opened her eyes.

She gets up and walks towards the kitchen with her lips curved into a knowing smile.

"You might as well make use of me being here." Joy, still topless, sits down next to me, cupping a glass of wine in her hands. "Shall I take you out later? Show you around?"

"Are you going to wear more clothes for that occasion?" There's bite to my tone. There's no way on earth

I would go into town with Joy, but her words do spark the hope that she'll go out later and leave me in peace for the rest of the evening.

"Does it bother you?" I can feel her eyes on me, but I stubbornly keep staring at the surface of the water. It's darker now that the sun is slanting down more. "I do apologise, Alice. I'm so used to it. It's more a reflex than anything else. Arrive at the house. Take off my top. It's just the way we roll here, always have."

"Do you mean to say that Miranda sits here like, uh, that as well?"

"Of course she does. It's really no big deal. It's just nature."

"Lord almighty," I whisper, trying hard not to imagine my oldest friend and business associate lowering herself gingerly into the pool with her chest bare. Thank goodness I never took her up on her offer to join her.

"If it makes you more comfortable I can put something on. I just didn't realise you would mind."

I'm torn. I don't want to be called uptight again. But not having to sit here and drink my wine with a topless woman in her twenties would allow me to relax more. "I would appreciate it." I turn my head and shoot her a quick smile.

"Ah well." Joy pushes herself out of her chair. "Your loss, Alice." She winks at me and, barefoot, wanders inside.

My loss? What is that supposed to mean? It's as though the girl has come here for one single reason: to wind me up.

A few minutes later she sits next to me in the same sheer tank top she arrived in, no bra underneath, and although it isn't much more than she had on before, it does ease some of the stiffness in my muscles. Before the subject of conversation again goes somewhere I don't want it to go, I hijack it, and start talking about work—always a safe topic.

"Miranda said something about you starting a new job soon?"

"Yep." Joy pulls her feet up onto the chair and rests her elbows on her knees. "Social media advertising. I'll mostly be working on Facebook ad campaigns."

I've heard of Facebook, of course, but I would never be caught dead on a platform like that. "Right," I say. "Sounds interesting."

Joy just chuckles, then says, "I don't want to talk about work, Alice. I'm on holiday." She lets her legs slide off the chair and deposits her—already—empty glass on the table in front of us. "So, are you game? We can either walk around the lake, or I can show you the shortcut to the beach, or we can just go for a drink in town, although 'town' is a big word for it."

"I'm not sure. I'd rather—"

"You have a date with Jack Reacher or something?" She cuts me off. "I was unfair to you earlier, by the way, I have read one or two Lee Childs—who hasn't?—and I even saw the movie, but, I mean, come on… Tom Cruise? For real?"

I'm not entirely sure what she's referring to, so I sit there mute.

This, apparently, is another good reason for Joy to start giggling. "Do you ever go to the movies?"

"Not very often."

"So what *do* you do for relaxation?" She twirls the stem of the wine glass between her fingers.

"I quite often go to plays and the opera. A museum once in a while on the weekend if there's an interesting exhibition. Much like your mother, I would think." I can't shake the feeling that I'm being questioned, that something about my personality or habits or the way I choose to live my life is under scrutiny.

"Mum? As far as I know she hasn't been to the opera for more than a decade, not since she met Jeff."

"Ah, Jeff."

Joy turns to me. "I never got a chance to ask you. You're one of Mum's best friends so you must have an opinion. What do you think of him?"

Miranda has been with Jeff for more than ten years. Any opinion I ever had about him—and I did have a few at the time—has become irrelevant. "They seem very happy together."

"That's not an answer to my question, Alice. Come on." She taps her fingertips onto the tabletop now. "Whatever is said here stays between us. I promise."

I inhale deeply before speaking. I don't even know if I can trust Joy because, as has become overly clear since her arrival earlier today, blood is always thicker than water. And, even though Miranda is my friend, we don't have the sort of relationship in which I would unabashedly voice my opinion on the dubious nature of the man in her life. "He's an acquired taste, I guess."

Joy shakes her head, a lopsided grin on her face. "Good thing I'm rather adept at deciphering middle-class social diplomacy." Out of nowhere, she puts a hand on my lower arm and pats it. I stare at the spot where she's touching me —openmouthedly, I realise too late. So much for social diplomacy. Joy retracts her hand. "He's a pompous, arrogant bastard. That's what he is." Joy looks me straight in the eyes. "Then again, so was my dad. At least Mum is consistent in her taste in men."

"Paul was no such thing."

"Oh come on, Alice. I know, I know. Don't speak ill of the dead and all that, but I'm his daughter, and very much like him when I come to think of it, so I'm allowed to speak my mind. Mum likes grandstanding men who are full of themselves. It's a fact."

I feel a bout of laughter rise within me, but I don't know if it's appropriate to chuckle at the memory of Joy's deceased father. "Obviously, you knew him much better than I did."

Joy rises to her feet. "How about we save our trip into town for tomorrow. I'll get some more snacks and wine and we can just stay here and chat?"

"You don't have to stay in on my account," I'm quick to say.

"It's no bother. I'm a bit tired from traveling anyway."

No bother? There goes my quiet evening. "Sure." I empty my glass of wine to mask any potential signs of disappointment on my face. While Joy goes inside to fetch the food and drinks, I remind myself to ask her, as soon as the occasion arises, when exactly her return flight is scheduled.

✶ ✶ ✶

"I can't believe this is your first time here, Alice," Joy says, after pouring me another glass of wine which I don't intend to touch a drop of.

"I'm not much of a traveller, I guess." I look out over the pool, now caught in shade.

"Still. It's barely three hours on a plane." Joy takes a sip, then continues. "My granny loved it when Mum bought the house. She came up here at least three times a year…"

"Is it really necessary to compare me to an OAP?" I have half a mind to scoot out of my chair and retreat back to my room, but it's a beautiful evening and I want to see the sun go down. Instead, I *do* drink from the wine—I bought it after all.

"I'm sorry, Alice. I didn't mean to do that." Joy has an amused expression on her face, as though she's taking great pleasure in winding me up. I have no doubt she is.

"I'm not so sure of that," I reply before grabbing a slice of the ham she deposited on the table. If I keep chugging back wine like this without eating anything, I'll pay for it in the morning.

"I swear to you. I'm on my best behaviour. Should I try to better it further?"

"You can do whatever you want." I start pushing back my chair, having changed my mind about watching the sunset. The sun has only gone down behind the trees and it will be a good while before we're given a glimpse of orange glow on the horizon. I can't wait that long—not in the company I'm currently in. "I'm going inside."

"What? No. Come on." Joy jumps out of her chair. "Let's try again, please. I know I'm an annoying brat." She cocks her head and protrudes her bottom lip. "Give me another chance?"

"If we're going to be sharing this house I expect to be treated respectfully." I sound like a headmistress scolding a child, which makes me feel utterly ridiculous.

"Nothing but respectful language from now on, I promise." Joy puts a hand on her chest, just above the curve of her breast, only attracting more attention to her see-through top.

"Fine," I say, but only because I think I may detect a glimmer of remorse in her eyes.

"It's not easy being this obnoxious all the time, you know," Joy says, then paints a smile on her face. "But none of us are perfect."

"That's certainly true." I cast her a severe glance before pulling my chair closer to the table again. We sit in silence for a while—a silence during which I feel compelled to empty half of my glass of wine. Though I'm grateful for the moment of quiet, the silence starts getting to me because it's awkward sitting next to someone and not making conversation.

"I'm glad I did finally make it here," I say, while twirling the stem of my glass between my fingers. "It's beautiful."

"I know." Joy has changed her tone of voice. It's gentler— less obnoxious. "I was so lucky to be able to come here as a child."

"Years ago, Alan did suggest we take a vacation here. I refused, as usual." And he started his affair with Sheryl not long after, I add in my head, while wondering how these words made their way out of my mouth. It must be the wine. I've had too much and it sneaked up on me.

"Do you mind me asking why?" Joy seems to have injected even more tenderness into her voice, and that edge of brashness she subjected me to earlier has disappeared altogether.

I glance at my almost empty glass of wine and, once again, vow to stop drinking from it. "Work," I say, then push my chair back again. "I'm going to get some water."

"Nope!" Joy is on her feet before me. "I'll get it. Sit back down." It's as though she's become scared I'll flee to my room and leave her to witness nightfall by herself.

While she's in the house I look up to the sky, to how it's starting to morph into that deep inky blue that sets the day apart from the night.

"Here you go." Joy has brought out a bottle of water and two glasses and makes a show of pouring us each one.

Despite knowing better, I drink from the water as though it has the capacity to dilute the alcohol level in my blood instantly. My cure for most things in life has almost always been abstinence, so I know I'm in trouble, having already far exceeded my daily unit limit. When I look at Joy I can see her straining to keep her mouth shut, as if it's chock-full and ready to burst with questions she wants to ask me.

"Spit it out," I say, curving *my* lips into an amused smile this time.

"What?" Joy asks. "The wine? No way, Alice. It's too good for that."

I burst out into a mild chuckle. "Whatever it is you want to ask me." Perhaps it's the relaxing atmosphere, or the sun dipping lower on the horizon, or too much wine consumed, or all of these things together, but, now that Joy has toned it down a bit, I'm actually beginning to enjoy this conversation. I've stepped so far out of my daily life, I might as well talk about a few things I barely even think about in London anymore.

"Okay." Joy eyes me while refilling our wine glasses. "So you'd rather work than take a holiday in this gorgeous place. That's interesting."

"That's not a question." Ostentatiously, I grab my wine glass and drink again—ignoring the vow I made earlier.

Joy chuckles. "Let me rephrase, Alice. Did you really prefer sitting in an office in rainy London over soaking up some lovely rays of sunshine in the Algarve with your then husband?" She looks at me triumphantly.

"Alan and I…" I start. "We lived our own lives. Or, at least, I did. Work was… *is* my life. That's why, in the end, I had to stop blaming him for leaving me for someone not only a lot younger than me, but willing to pay more attention to him." After saying those words out loud, I actually need another sip of wine.

"That's very honest of you." The triumphant smile has left Joy's lips. She probably didn't expect me to open up about Alan so much. Truth be told, nor did I. Joy's effect on me seems to be changing exponentially the more wine I drink. While sunlight has given way to approaching darkness, she has somehow transformed herself from an aggravating presence into an easy conversation partner.

"It's the truth, though I didn't see it that way when he left me." I eye both the glasses in front of me and opt for the water this time. I suddenly dread having to get up, afraid I won't be able to make it to my bedroom in a straight line.

"Hindsight and all that," Joy says. She stares into her wineglass gloomily, giving me the impression she's reminiscing about her own amorous past—or present.

When I close my eyes briefly, my head starts to spin. As soon as I open them, I reach for the water glass again and gulp down the remaining liquid.

"I take it you're not a heavy drinker," Joy says, as she refills my water glass.

"I can enjoy a good glass of wine, but other than that, I don't have much use for alcohol in my life." I slap my palms onto the armrests of my chair a bit more heavily than expected. "Speaking of which—alcohol I mean—I believe it may have got the better of me. I really do need to go and lie down now." By the time I make it out of my chair, I'm actually a little sad to leave Joy to enjoy the rest of the evening by herself.

"Will you be okay?" Joy asks with a hint of worry in her voice.

"Certainly," I say, though my legs feel a bit wobbly. "Good night, Joy. See you tomorrow." Instead of heading towards the French windows of my bedroom, I take the longer, inside route, through the kitchen, just so Joy doesn't have to witness me staggering drunkenly, and very un-ladylike, along the patio.

CHAPTER FOUR

I wake up the next day with my brain banging against my skull and the foulest taste in my mouth. The sun comes through the windows—I didn't even close the curtains. I bring my hands to my head and start to massage my temples, as if it will make any difference. I more than exceeded my two units last night. When I gently move my head to the left and my gaze catches the alarm clock I am appalled that it's past 10 a.m. What on earth got into me? How many more days before Joy leaves? I might have asked her last night, but if I did I don't recall the answer.

By the time I manage to get out of bed, take a long, cold shower and put some clothes on, I find Joy in the kitchen brewing coffee.

"The lady has awoken," she says.

I don't know why, but I feel my cheeks flush at her comment—even though she's wearing her bikini *with* top this morning. "You're a bad influence, young lady."

"I'll take the blame." She points at the coffee machine. "Some of this and a Panadol and you'll be good as new."

I shake my head. "I don't take unnecessary medication."

"Of course you don't." That knowing smile again. "But I bet you don't usually have more than a couple of glasses of wine either. I would call these extraneous circumstances, Alice. Plus, you only have so many days here, don't waste one on a hangover you can easily cure."

"Gosh, why didn't *you* become a lawyer? You certainly have the mouth for it."

"I feel responsible for your physical state, so let me take care of you, okay?" Undeterred, she pours a mug of steaming coffee and hands it to me. "Why don't you take this out on the patio and I'll bring you everything you need."

"I'll be fine—"

"No buts. Go on." Joy actually has the nerve to pat me on the small of my back and coax me in the direction of the terrace. I have no energy to fight her. I missed the early morning coolness and it's already hot and muggy in the shade of the patio. I sit down in the same chair as the night before, and just the act of being in the same spot triggers a figment of a memory. Did I talk about Alan?

"Here you go." She deposits a big bottle of water and a box of painkillers on the table. "There's more coffee if you want it. I'll make a quick run to the shop and get us some much needed brunch ingredients. A swim can work wonders as well to make you feel human again."

Just watching Joy and her boundless energy makes my head hurt again. "How are you feeling?"

"Perfectly fine. I can handle more than a bottle of wine." She shrugs. "Do you need anything else from the shop?"

I can't remember the last time someone else did my shopping for me. "No, thank you."

"Okay." Joy quickly walks inside, grabs her purse and car keys. "I'm cooking tonight, by the way. I want to make amends."

"Are you going to the supermarket dressed like that?"

"Sure."

I let my gaze wander over her body, and wonder if she's doing this to deliberately antagonise me—even though I know, deep down, she's not. The colour of her bikini is hot pink and it barely covers the essentials. I refrain from shaking my head. At least she's not wearing flip-flops to drive.

While Joy is away I take one of the Panadols and wash

it down with as much water as my stomach will hold. Then, while my eyes follow a tiny bird that hops up and down the side of the pool, I ask myself if I had a good time last night. Reluctantly, I agree that I did. Despite the brusque in-your-face nature of Joy's arrival, and her bratty retorts, and her overall directness regarding just about everything, she's not too bad to have as company. It could have been worse. She could have brought a boyfriend, or a friend, and have made me feel completely obsolete.

By the time Joy returns with eggs, bread, cheese and bacon, my headache has mostly retreated.

"How are we feeling?" Joy asks as I stand up to give her a hand. Joy immediately wags a finger at me, not waiting for my reply. "Nu-uh! Sit back down, please. I'm nothing if not a woman of my word. I got you drunk, now I will nurse your hangover. That's how I roll."

Meekly, I fall back into my chair, admitting to myself that having things done for me—even the simple act of making breakfast—is rather nice.

The eggs Joy serves me are just right, not dry and not overly runny either.

"How's that for service?" she asks, once my plate is clean.

"I could get used to it," I concede.

"You have me for three more days. I've already told you to make the most of it." Joy flashes me one of her toothy grins. "I take it you won't be venturing out today?"

I've been here two days and I've barely left Miranda's property.

"Pool and Jack Reacher for you?" She goes on. "I honestly don't mind. I could do with the same myself, minus Jack, that is." She winks at me and starts clearing the table, without me even having responded to any of her questions.

✶ ✶ ✶

"Gin o'clock," Joy says when the pool is bathed in shade. "Would you care for one?"

I've spent my day alternately dozing in the shadow of a large tree and gingerly taking dips in the pool—not swimming for exercise but for recovery. "Heavens no."

"Are you sure? I hate drinking alone." Joy has taken off her top again, claiming that tan lines are 'so nineties'.

"I'm positive." Between slumbers, I've seen her dive in and push herself out of the pool, and I guess I'm becoming used to her state of undress. It seems to bother me less and less. "I'm going to dress for dinner."

"There's really no need. It's just us and I'm not planning on putting on my dinner jacket."

"Need or not," I push myself out of my sun lounger, "it's how I like it."

In my room, I peel my bathing suit off me, and ponder wearing the bikini I brought tomorrow. I look at my reflection in the mirror. I'm certainly in much better shape than Miranda. I never understood how other people can be so careless with their bodies, drinking countless units of alcohol, eating fried food, and failing to exercise at least four times a week.

"I don't have time to occupy myself with all of that, Alice," Miranda said once when I had questioned her about the topic. "I have a bloody life to live."

Joy, who seems to easily slip into a southern European lifestyle, has consumed at least three G&Ts—as far as I can tell—by the time she serves dinner at ten to nine. By then, I've sat at the table in linen trousers and a freshly-ironed top for an hour and a half, patiently waiting while sipping sparkling water.

"Here you go, Madam," she says, as she plants a—I must admit—divine looking plate of food in front of me. "Salmon à la Jamie Oliver with crushed potatoes and minted greens."

"You're quite the little chef." I look into Joy's brown eyes for an instant and see no evidence of the three cocktails she has already consumed.

"Can I serve you some chilled white wine with that? It's a local one. Very easy on the palate."

Despite myself, and my reluctance to drink anything but water, I chuckle at the mock-posh tone of her voice.

"I'll take that as a yes." Joy heads back inside and brings out a bottle of wine stuffed into a cool bag.

"You're a really bad influence on me." While I take a sip of the wine I look into her eyes again and see how they glimmer with mischief.

"You have enough margin of error for that. I hardly think you'll leave here a bad girl, Alice." Joy holds my gaze for a few seconds. I can't help but smile again.

"This is absolutely delicious. Who taught you how to cook?"

"Certainly not Mum. I spent a lot of time in the kitchen with Dad before he got too sick. After that, I guess I just taught myself. There are entire YouTube channels dedicated to teaching people how to cook. Countless apps with recipes. I sometimes wonder how anyone learned in the olden days."

"The olden days? You mean when I was younger?" By now, I know she's goading me, and I play along.

"Well, you didn't have the internet when you were learning how to cook."

"We didn't have it and we didn't need it. How many hours today did you spend glued to your mobile phone? It seemed as though every time I opened my eyes, you were entranced by it."

"Checking up on me, were you?"

It's sudden remarks like this that make me feel most ill at ease. Nevertheless, I raise my eyebrows and wait for her response.

"I can tell you exactly because there is an app for that." Joy reaches for her phone, touches the screen a few times, then shows it to me. "Two hours and forty-five minutes," she says. "A bit much, I must admit, but I am on holiday and

Candy Crush isn't going to play itself." She puts her phone to the side. "Maybe I'll go on a digital fast. But then you will have to entertain me, Alice. You can start by picking up the story about Alan where you left it last night."

"I'm afraid I have no recollection of that," I lie. During the course of the afternoon, snippets of conversation have come back to me.

"You can't fool me. Granted, you can't hold your liquor, but you didn't drink *that* much."

"Maybe not, but I really don't feel like devoting any more time to talking about my ex-husband."

"Fair enough." For a good few minutes, the only sounds are made by us eating. Since she arrived and we've been in each other's company, I haven't known her to be quiet for this long.

"I'd react the same way if you asked me about my ex. Alex is one of the reasons I wanted to come down here, away from everything and everyone in London."

Miranda never mentions Joy's boyfriends, so this is the first I hear about Alex. "Did he leave you for someone half his age as well?"

Joy huffs out a breathy chuckle. "Hardly." She puts down her fork. "And Alex is not a he. All woman last time I checked."

"Oh." Now I'm truly stumped. I have known Miranda for thirty years. We've been business partners for twenty-five. Never has she given me the slightest tidbit of information about her only child's sexual preference.

"You didn't know?" Joy falls back into her chair, an amused smile playing on her lips. "That doesn't surprise me. She hasn't fully accepted it yet. I really don't know why she has such a hard time with it. To her credit, I only came out two years ago, and sometimes it takes time for parents to readjust their ideas about their children and their dreams for them. I do get that." The carefreeness that has characterised Joy's tone of voice seems to have disappeared for the first time. She pulls up her shoulders. "For now, she just refuses to talk about it, but I think she'll come round in the end."

"I'm so sorry. I had absolutely no idea."

"We haven't fallen out. I mean, she still does my laundry every week for Christ's sake. She'll wash my knickers but won't talk about my love life. How's that for good old Britishness?"

"Were you and, uh, Alex together for a long time?"

"Nah, just a few months. It was never going to be serious. I'm not that cut-up about it, either way. I just needed a break from everything. Clear my head before I start this new job, you know?"

I nod, despite not knowing at all.

"So, thank you very much for allowing me to come over. Did Mum have to be very persuasive? I know you value your privacy. I want you to know that I really appreciate you letting me crash your holiday."

"I was reluctant at first. I've lived alone for a very long time and am quite set in my ways, but it's quite… fun to have you around." I'm surprised by my own words. Perhaps Joy's tiny display of vulnerability has increased my liking of her. And she has utterly spoiled me today.

"How about some night swimming then?"

"What?" She keeps doing this, keeps springing the most improbable suggestions on me when I least expect it.

"That's why I don't bother dressing up for dinner. The lure of the water is too great after dark. We can take a torch and head over to the beach. I promise you, it'll be glorious."

"Erm, I really don't think so, Joy." I start collecting our plates.

"Just come with me to the beach then. It's so special this time of the day. So quiet, and I know just the spot for some privacy. I've been coming here a long time. I want to show you. It'll be an adventure." Joy quirks her eyebrows into a strangely touching quizzical shape. She has my sympathy now, and I find it hard to say no.

"Fine, but I'm not going into the water."

✳ ✳ ✳

The short-cut to the beach proves to be an uneven dirt path full of dangerously loose stones and tricky little dips. En route, I scold myself for being so unwise as to being fooled into doing this after dark. Joy uses her phone as a guiding light while I carefully pick my way to the beach with a proper torch—although the illumination it provides is not nearly enough for the rough terrain I find myself on.

"Almost there," Joy says. She's leading the way, balancing a beach bag with a couple of towels and a bottle of wine she insisted on taking. She's wearing a bright white t-shirt with nothing underneath and a pair of bikini bottoms. I'm still in my dinner outfit from earlier.

Just as extreme fatigue, a leftover from this morning's hangover, hits me, Joy stops, and says, "Ta-dah!"

But it's too dark to see anything, really, except black sea on black beach. I'm not immediately sure what is so spectacular about this. Watching Joy dart onto the beach also makes me wonder what the hell I'm doing here. This is something young people do, when they are still brazen and spontaneous. I haven't been either in a very long time.

Still, I'm here now. So I follow Joy onto the beach. My sandals instantly fill with sand—and I remember why I'm not a beach person. When I reach the spot where Joy has set up camp, two towels spread out next to each other, she's already taking off her top.

Just as she tosses her t-shirt onto the towel, she glares at me, her eyes shiny in the night, and says, "I'm doing you a courtesy, Alice. When there's absolutely no one around like tonight, I'd usually take off my bottoms as well."

"Well, then," is all I can say.

"Do yourself a small favour," Joy continues, "roll up those trousers and at least dip your toes in the water." She cocks her head and stands there looking at me for an instant, her hands at her waist. Her chest rises and falls quickly.

"All right." Because what else am I going to do? Sit here on my own in the dark?

Joy doesn't wait for me. In a flash, she's off, out of my sight, swallowed by the darkness of the night.

I roll up my trousers, as instructed, take the torch, and head towards the water. The roar of the waves drowns out any other sound there might be, but it's just us here tonight, and I let my torch train over the water, looking for Joy. She's diving into the waves, pinching her nostrils shut with her fingers as she goes under, doing a somersault before emerging from the sea. Perhaps I'm in a poetic mood, but the image strikes me as one of pure, uninhibited happiness. I remember myself at twenty-nine—already so serious, so consumed with work. I would never have ducked into a wave like that.

Joy has had enough of somersaulting and heads towards me. The closer she gets, the less of her is covered by the water, and the sight of her shocks me. It's nothing I haven't seen before—Joy all wet, drops of water raining down her bare breasts. But the emptiness of the beach, and the water immersing my ankles and then retreating, the repetitive motion of it somehow soothes me. And that funny feeling, one I haven't experienced in decades, when a hangover is finally flushed from the body. The unexpected pleasure I've taken in Joy's company. All of these strangely converge within me and make my stomach tingle. As if the sight of Joy walking towards me like that is one I've been waiting for my entire life. Embarrassed, I look away, and gaze at the stars, which are plenty, while I wait for this foolishness to flee my brain.

"Aren't you bummed that you didn't bring your bathing suit now?" Joy presses water drops from her long hair with a backwards movement of her hands, pushing her chest forward.

"Hm," I hum, trying to hide my discomfort.

"Just take off your clothes, Alice. There's no one here. I

won't look, I promise." She shoots me a wink, and I'm not the sort of person who can respond to this playfully.

"I think I'll head back. You enjoy yourself."

"What? No. No, no, no." Joy takes a few more steps towards me, the water splashing up around her legs. "Stay. I lugged that bottle of wine all the way down here. You know I hate drinking alone."

"I'm very sorry, Joy. I'd really rather head back. I'm tired. I want to go to sleep."

"What's wrong?"

It's absurd to have this conversation here, both our feet in the water, waves rolling in around us. "Nothing." But I can't stay. Not after that unsettling sense of losing control over something I've been holding onto—perhaps ever since Alan left me, or perhaps since forever—sneaked up on me.

"I'll go back with you then. Just let me dry off."

"No, really, it's fine." I need to be alone. Walk it off. Have the house to myself for a little while—at least long enough to shake this off without Joy's noises filtering through my bedroom wall.

"Be careful then." Joy touches her fingertips to my upper arm. It's the second time today she has done something like that. I'm not used to that at all.

"I will. Good night." I turn around, secretly dreading the walk back on my own, but I don't have a choice now.

CHAPTER FIVE

When I hear the knock on my door at a quarter past nine, I have been awake for hours, but I have been afraid to get up and face Joy.

"Alice? Are you awake?"

I shuffle upwards, straightening my nightie. "Yes. Not to worry," I shout.

"Can I come in?"

I cover as much of myself as I can with the sheet. "Sure, but I'm fine."

The door opens and Joy's head peeks through. "Do I owe you an apology? Was it something I said or did?" She accompanies her words with a goofy grin. "I shouldn't have insisted you take off your clothes. I realise that now." She pushes the door open farther and leans against the frame. She's wearing a flimsy tank top, barely worth the name, that covers only her breasts and nothing of her belly. Her skin has already turned darker, and it seems to shine with youth.

"Always the uptight one," I joke, desperate to change the topic. "Does your offer to show me around still stand? I would love to explore the area a bit."

"Yes! I know just where to take you. Are you okay to drive? I know myself. I'll want to have a drink on the way and I don't want to chauffeur you around when I do."

"No problem."

"Eggs?"

"I can make my own, but thank you for asking."

"Let's aim to leave around eleven? There's fresh coffee in the kitchen."

★ ★ ★

"You're one of Mum's very best friends, yet I hardly know you," Joy says, while fiddling with her phone, trying to connect it to the car's bluetooth system.

We've been driving for a good half hour on our way to Sagres and all the radio stations quickly proved inadequate for Joy.

"Ah! I think it's working. What are you in the mood for? Some Bruce Springsteen?"

I shoot Joy a glance. I had expected her to just put on some deafening dance music.

"I happen to love Bruce Springsteen."

"Yeah?" There's surprise in her voice. "What's your favourite album?"

"*Nebraska*," I say, without hesitation.

"Gloomy." Within seconds, the mouth organ of the album's title song starts playing.

"You have my favourite record readily available on your phone?"

"What can I say? I like old things," Joy says.

I have my eyes focused on the road, but I can hear the smile in her voice. "Mind you, if you'd requested Neil Diamond or Tom Jones, I wouldn't have complied so easily."

"Decidedly too sappy."

"I'm so glad we agree." Joy puts her phone in the space between our seats and her elbow briefly brushes against mine. "But back to my earlier question. How come you hardly ever came round when I was still living with Mum?"

I sigh. "I did. In the beginning. But after my divorce, Miranda got obsessed with setting me up with one of her friends, kept inviting me round for dinner parties I was loathe to attend, so I just stopped coming, I guess."

"Oh Christ. Who did she thrust in your face? Wait… let me guess. Lionel? She's been trying to pawn him off for as long as I can remember."

"Lionel Ashley. That's correct. A nice enough man, but

really not my type. In any way."

"Really, Alice? The man has such a lovely high-pitched voice, and that head of lush hair. How could you possibly have resisted?" Joy's laugh is infectious.

Once she has settled down, I continue my explanation. "Then Miranda started seeing Jeff and there were fewer and fewer dinner parties. Either way, we see each other at work every day. There needs to be some distance."

"Hm. Yeah." Joy turns up the volume dial. "This is truly one of the best songs ever made."

"I completely agree."

"Have you ever seen him live?" she asks.

"No. I never was much of a concert goer."

"I have. In Atlantic City in 2005. It was just… mind-blowing," Joy says while her head sways to the melody.

"You sure do get around." It's a pity we're having this conversation in the car and I need to keep my eyes on the road. I'd love to see Joy's facial expressions.

"Well, we all can't be homebodies like you, Alice. The economy would go bust."

"I contribute plenty to the economy."

"Oh yeah? When did you last splash out on something?"

"I'm on holiday in the Algarve," I retort.

"That doesn't count. Surely, Mum didn't make you pay?"

"She didn't. I wanted to, but she refused." I shake my head. "I contribute to the economy by paying a lot of taxes."

"You should spoil yourself more. On their death bed, no one has ever wished they'd worked more." Joy sounds just like Miranda.

"That's a bit grim."

"Perhaps, but it's also true." A short silence descends. "Take last night, for instance. Why didn't you join me? Let your hair down a bit? There was no one to judge you but yourself."

"Last night…" I try to come up with a decent explanation. "I was tired. And I would never, not in a million years, go into the sea in just my underwear. It's not even conceivable."

"Why not?"

"Because… I'm not that kind of person."

"What kind of person? The kind that enjoys life?"

I make an elaborate play of overtaking a van that has been driving at a maddeningly slow pace in front of us for miles, hoping the topic will just die. I don't feel like defending myself for simply being who I am.

"I'm not attacking you, Alice. I swear. I'm just trying to understand."

"You and I are very different people. I grew up in a time when everything was different. Unlike you, I wasn't raised with the belief that the world was my oyster."

I can feel Joy's stare boring into me, but I keep looking straight ahead. "I understand that we're different and from other generations and all that, but, come on, my own mum is older than you and she's very prone to some hedonism. So, in my humble opinion, it's definitely not just a generational issue."

"Of course not. Everyone is different." And I know all about Miranda's hedonism—and the number of days she's taken off because of it since we went into business together. But Miranda's life has always been the opposite of mine.

"Mum will kill me if she ever finds out I told you this, but we used to have a running joke in our house. Whenever one of us didn't feel like doing a chore, we'd say 'Better call Alice' because, even when Mum was absent from work, you'd still get everything done. Mind you, apart from the joke, Mum has the greatest respect for you. She really appreciates everything you've done for her over the years. I know that much."

"It works both ways." I'm not at all offended by Miranda's family's joke, more flattered than anything, really.

"Jones & McAllister is our law firm, but from the very beginning, I've had to call all the shots, which has allowed me a degree of control I probably wouldn't have had otherwise."

"And let me guess… Alice McAllister likes being in control." Joy chuckles. "By the way, you have me to thank for that. If I hadn't been born when I was, your life might be totally different. You basically owe me, Alice."

"I don't believe a person owes another anything simply because they exist." Perhaps my voice is more serious than I want it to sound.

"I was only joking," Joy says quickly. "Oh, hold on. If we go off the main road here, I know just the spot for lunch."

✶ ✶ ✶

After a delicious meal of cataplana and grilled squid, during which Joy somehow manages to consume three Portuguese beers, which she claims were not strong at all, we approach our destination.

The wind is fierce, bringing the temperature way down, and I feel a chill on my skin as I exit the car. This drop in temperature doesn't seem to affect Joy at all, as she bounds out of the car, nearly jumping up and down with excitement, the way a child would. "This is one of my top spots in the whole wide world. There's just something about it. But you have to see it to believe it."

I follow her to a curvy white building that looks a bit like a church. All around us we're surrounded by the bluest of water. We walk through a courtyard with some stalls selling coffee and souvenirs, then end up in front of one of the most stunning views I've ever come across. Blue can't describe the colour of the water, nor of the sky. It's like a condensed version of all the existing blues in the world, intensified by the white of the building flanking the ocean on the top of the cliff where we're standing.

"Bottom left corner of Europe," Joy says. "This can

only mean one thing: selfie time."

For the first time since she arrived, and despite having had many an occasion to do so already, I roll my eyes at her. "You go ahead, dear." I mean to sound every bit as condescending as I do.

"Just one picture of the two of us?" Joy looks at me like a toddler who wants to beg one more sweet from her parents after they've already closed the packet.

For the life of me, I can't refuse her. "All right then."

"Brilliant. Come on." She opens one arm wide, indicating where I should stand. Her other hand holds the phone at arm's length.

I step into her half-embrace, and she clutches my shoulder with her fingers, pulling me close to her. Her body heat is welcome in the brisk wind that blows our hair in all directions. I can feel the side of her breast press into me, and the same sensation as last night—the one I ran away from so ungracefully—hits me with full force again.

"Smile!" Joy says.

I try, but I'm not keen to see the result.

"Okay, we're going to have to do another because you look as though I'm pinching your arse in this one," Joy says.

"I don't photograph well," I say, scolding myself for letting myself be talked into having a 'selfie' taken. I mean, really.

"This one's much better." Joy lets go of my shoulder, but not without giving it a gentle squeeze first. "Look." She shows me the phone screen, but the sun is too bright and I'm glad I can't really see the photo.

"Hm," is all I say, but Joy is busy on her phone anyway.

"Let me just upload it to Facebook. You can have one guess as to who will be the first person to 'Like' it."

"I have no earthly idea." I turn to take in the view some more. The ruggedness of the ocean, the vastness of it, allows me to put what I'm feeling into perspective. Either way, it's of no importance. Just some stress release mingling with the frivolity of being on the road with someone so much younger than me, and with such a different view of the world. It's no wonder I'm a bit shaken.

"Mum, of course. She's even worse than I am."

"Miranda is on Facebook?"

"Yep, and she's what? Seven years older than you? Eight?"

"Meaning?"

"Nothing, Alice." Joy bumps her shoulder into mine. "Anyway, all the younger people are moving onto Instagram these days now that their grandparents are all on Facebook." A vibrating sound stops Joy mid-speech. "Ah, here she is already." She unlocks her phone by holding her thumb on a button at the bottom. "What did I say? Here, check this." Joy thrusts the phone in my direction and I see a comment below the picture of Joy and me:

Beautiful picture. Glad you two are getting along. Alice: don't forget to relax!

"Instant attention and gratification," I say, pushing the 'getting along' part of the comment to the back of my brain as quickly as possible. "Is that why these, uh, technologies are so popular?"

"It's just a bit of fun. And it keeps Mum happy that she can follow me around—at least she thinks she does. You should see my Instagram account."

Despite myself, my curiosity is piqued. "You'll have to show it to me then."

Joy clearly wasn't expecting that reply. "I will. Tonight. Promise." She draws her eyes into slits as she scans my face.

"When did you come here last?" I ask, eager for a change of subject, and to not have Joy look at me anymore the way she's doing now.

"Not too long ago. I make a point of coming here every time I visit Portugal. There's something about standing at the edge of the world that, I don't know, frees me of all the bullshit that life brings. The wind. The azure of the sea.

The pureness of it. It levels me somehow."

I can fully relate to Joy's words. She's not that much of a brat then.

"Dad loved it here as well. We used to come here, just the two of us. Stay for hours while, usually, tourists tend to come and go pretty quickly. We'd have a coffee or an ice cream, then, sometimes, crawl down those rocks there." She points to her right, to a precarious spot on the slope of the hill where a brave fisherman has set up.

"You went down there? How did you manage that?"

"Fearlessness, I guess. And a little arrogance. Definitely the Perkins side of the family."

I can imagine Paul clambering down. It does sound like something he would have done. "Can I buy you an ice cream?" I offer.

"Only if we climb down afterwards," Joy says.

My limbs stiffen at the thought.

"Only kidding." Joy flashes me a wide smile. "But I will have that ice cream."

On the way back, Joy nods off. Before she drifted off into sleep, she put on *Darkness on the Edge of Town* and I hum along to the lyrics, surprising myself by remembering the full chorus and singing along to it without hesitation. Out of the wind, and with the steady thrum of the car, I feel a drowsiness settling in my bones despite the two espressos I drank before we left, and this day out has given me a new kind of energy. A buzz humming underneath my skin, like a neon light flickering to life. Only four more days with Joy, I find myself thinking. Whatever will I do with myself when she's gone?

CHAPTER SIX

After dinner, Joy initiates me into the secrets of Instagram. She shows me picture after picture—all of them spectacular-looking and boasting amazing colours—of her in various spots in London. One at Miranda's house. One at a bar called Sax in East London. One of her cuddling an adorably fluffy puppy.

"This is Alex," she says, when we reach a picture of her and another woman.

I had expected someone similar in age to Joy and, perhaps also, similar in looks, but the woman in the picture looks nothing like Joy. For starters, she's at least in her late thirties, if not early forties, and is dressed up in a pants suit and crisply ironed blouse.

"Wow," I say.

"What's that supposed to mean?"

I sense a small shift in Joy's energy, like she's going on the defence—like a secret has been unearthed.

"She's not what I had expected, that's all."

"What *had* you expected?" Joy puts the phone on the table.

"Gosh, I really don't know. Like you said earlier in the car, we barely know each other, so it's hard to say."

She reaches for the bottle of wine and pours herself another glass—I stopped keeping count a few hours ago, quickly realising there's no point.

"I'm sorry. It's just that you really sounded a lot like Mum just then." She gazes into the dark liquid in her glass.

"How so?" It's only natural though, I think, considering

my connection to Miranda—and how close in age we are.

"When I told her about Alex, she said the exact same thing. That she wasn't what she had expected." At last, Joy drinks.

"Because she's older than you? Or because she's a woman?"

Joy sets her glass down and rubs her palms over her forehead. "She was my boss. It was bad judgement on both our parts. I quit, so she didn't have to fire me."

I'm not a keen watcher of soap operas, but this is beginning to sound like one. "Christ." I'm also beginning to think that Miranda might not have such an issue with her daughter's sexual preference as with her taste in partners. "Was she your, uh, first, uh, female partner?"

"God no. I started dating women when I was at UCLA. It was so easy to hide it from Mum. She wasn't on Facebook yet back then." There's room for a small chuckle. "I only told her when I moved back to London and I started seeing someone seriously. She didn't approve of Tamsin either, even though she was a barrister."

I'm starting to understand why people enjoy dramatic television so much: to completely let go of their own woes and focus on someone else's is so liberating for the mind. I do, however, notice that Joy is in distress. For someone so confident and loud-mouthed at first sight, she's struggling to find the words now.

"How old was Tamsin?" I might be wrong, but I think I may have detected a pattern.

"Thirty-six at the time. Really not that much older than me."

I quickly do the calculation in my head—and disagree. "What happened? Why did it end?" I might as well know it all now.

"She had huge problems with the fact that I was still living with Mum at my age. But I was only twenty-six and had just moved back to the UK. Personally, I think that's completely understandable, what with the ludicrous rental prices and all that. I was just taking my time after leaving the States. Just chilling a bit before finding a job. In the end, it felt more like having two mothers."

"I'm so sorry, Joy." I empty my own glass of wine. I have a burning question on my mind, but need more liquid courage before I can even contemplate asking it.

"Oh, it's fine. I'm not really looking for anything serious, anyway. I'd prefer to get settled in my new job first." She pulls up her shoulders. "Coming here was a good idea, although I hadn't expected to have these sorts of conversations with you, Alice, I must admit."

"I've always been a good listener."

"And you like Bruce Springsteen." Under the table, she bumps her knee against mine. "But enough about me, let's talk about you. How long have you been divorced? Ages right? Since before I left for the States. You must have had some romance in your life after Alan?"

"Not really." I'm so unaccustomed to speaking about my own feelings, I had thought it would be more difficult. "Lionel certainly didn't float my boat." I admit to myself that I'm trying to elicit a snort from her. "There was this solicitor from Chauncey & Wagner who took me out on a few dates. His name was Pierre, although he wasn't French, but I guess I wasn't forthcoming enough to keep him interested."

"Goodness, Alice, what do you mean by that? You didn't put out?" Joy is giggling now.

"I honestly don't know, but that's how I label it. To put my mind at ease. But, if I'm truly honest, I just didn't want another Alan. We didn't have the best marriage, but certainly not the worst I've seen either. When he left me, simply discarded me for that woman, it hurt to become this huge cliché. It wasn't just that he left, and I was alone, but it wounded my pride also, and it left me deeply sceptical of humans in general."

Joy is no longer chuckling. "Well, fuck him, Alice. Really, fuck him."

"It's all a bit more complex than just him leaving me for someone ten years younger than me. Other factors were in play, to give him a little bit of credit."

"Fuck credit, Alice. He doesn't deserve it."

"He's not a monster. He's the man I married. The person I believed I'd spend the rest of my life with, but really, there are no guarantees simply because you exchange vows in front of your friends and family. As soon as I'd signed the divorce papers, I knew I would never marry again. But now, fifteen years later, I don't blame him for leaving me. We should have been more open with each other before we married, but back then, people got married so young just to be able to move out of their parents' house. I'm surely to blame as well."

"Relationships are complicated." Joy puts her feet on the chair opposite. "Although I do believe that they don't necessarily have to be. I think the less complicated, the more chance of success. Even though, of course, I hardly have the track record to prove my theory. Or, in fact, I do. Every relationship I've ever had, has always been too complicated. It was never as simple as girl liking girl, falling in love, building a life together. I often ask myself why, you know? Why do I fall for these women whom, in hindsight, I should have so easily suspected of not being a good fit for me?"

"You're young, Joy. You're learning, discovering your likes and dislikes. I think it's good that you haven't settled down yet. But, erm…" I'm glad the candle in the middle of the table is dying so the blush on my cheeks is hidden.

"What?" Joy has finished her glass of wine again. Perhaps Miranda should be more worried about the amount of wine her daughter can put away than about the age of her suitors. "No need to be shy anymore now, Alice."

"You do seem to have a propensity for falling for older women."

Joy just cocks her head in acquiescence. "True. I do. Even in college I was always lusting after my professors instead of my roommates. It's been like that for as long as I can remember being interested in other people amorously and… sexually. I don't really know how to explain it, but I find older women so much sexier than women my own age, let alone younger ones. It's just my preference, I guess. I'm a real cougar lover, me."

"A what?" I'm confused again. I thought we were discussing Joy's liking of more mature ladies, not wildlife.

"God, Alice." She throws her head back in mock-desperation. "You really are so *not* down with popular culture." She looks at me again. "A cougar is an older woman who devours younger men or women. I'm the opposite of a cougar, I guess, although I'm not sure there's a name for that."

"Someone who likes old meat. Hm, I'll have to think about that." The things I've learnt today. Perhaps I will have to start believing what Miranda sometimes says to me: that an entire world is passing me by because I work too much.

"*Quid pro quo?*" Joy asks. I do know what *that* means, although I'm not sure I like the implication of it. "I've answered your question as honestly as I could, can I ask you one in return?"

"Will I need another glass of wine to comply with your request?" I reach for the bottle already, knowing full well that Joy won't ask me an innocent question.

"Good plan." She holds out her own glass as well. I divide what is left of the bottle between us.

"I don't mean to be indiscreet, but you just said that you and Alan split fifteen years ago, and that you haven't really dated since."

"That's correct," I say, before sipping from the wine.

"So you haven't had sex with anyone in fifteen years?" Joy's voice is surprisingly low and solemn.

"Also correct."

Joy is silent, but at least she doesn't send me a look of pity, the way Miranda used to do back in the days when she was still trying to get me off the shelf. "Don't you miss it?"

"*Miss* is definitely not the correct word. I miss intimacy, and touching someone just because you want to and you love them, but to say that I miss having sex, would be a lie."

Joy sits up and rubs two fingers across her chin. "Was Alan that bad?"

I burst into laughter. She giggles with me. After the ripples of laughter subside, a silence descends upon us.

"All jokes aside." Joy fills the silence. "I'm by nature quite a tactile person, what with having spent so much time in LA, the city of hugs—sincere and, more often, otherwise —and I do have the habit of inadvertently touching people around me. I've noticed how surprised you've been by that."

"It's okay. But I'm *touched* that you would bring it up."

"Ha, good one." She lets her feet drop off the other chair and turns towards me. "But, just for the record, it's a damn shame that you're not having sex, Alice. And not just because you have a killer body for a woman in her fifties."

I decide not to take offence. It's easier than I thought. "It's a gradual process. It's not as though, fifteen years ago, I decided to stop having sex. I had to take the time to 'de-Alan' first, and digest my broken marriage. Then, in the beginning, I was on the look-out, which led to my platonic affair with Pierre, and after that, I started looking—and caring—less and less. I'm not an unhappier person because of it. I have my work, to which, Miranda repeats often enough, I am as good as married. I've never really felt as though I'm missing anything."

Joy drinks again and her stare gets bolder. "Okay, ask me a another question, Alice, because I can think of a few more for you."

"It doesn't have to be tit for tat. Now that I've told you all of this already, I have no qualms about telling you more," I say.

"No, I like it this way. And I also feel like unburdening myself some more. God, it feels good to just sit here and talk. I don't do enough of that back home."

"Okay, let me think." But I don't have to think for very long. There's so much I want to know about Joy now that we've started sharing. "When did you know that you liked women?"

"That was predictable." She smiles and leans her chin on her upturned palms. "It wasn't a big aha-moment, more like a culmination of conclusions. It all added up in my mind by the time I left for college. But as for when I really *knew*, I guess that was just before my eighteenth birthday. School had just ended, as had my guitar lessons with Miss Stevenson. I realised I wasn't going to be seeing her anymore, and I nearly wanted to cancel my enrolment at UCLA just at the thought of it."

"Teacher crush?"

"Oh God… the worst!" Joy straighens, and draws her feet up on the chair the way she always does. "Once I arrived in LA, I got over it quickly enough, though."

"Your turn," I say, while wishing I'd had another glass of wine.

"Okay, but just so I know how to play my cards here, how much longer are we doing this for, because I have at least two pertinent questions remaining."

"Two is fine." I can't remember the last time I shared so much extremely private information about myself with someone else.

Joy paints a smile on her lips. The candle on the table has died and all that illuminates us is a faint porch light on the wall behind me. "Okay, the easy one first." She sinks her teeth into her bottom lip before she speaks. "Seeing as, after Alan, you didn't appear to be very interested in pursuing anything with men, have you ever considered women?"

My eyebrows shoot up, my mouth falls open. "Honestly, with my hand on my heart: no, I haven't."

"Why not? I mean, I know I'm very biased, but in my eyes, relationship-wise there's nothing designed to work better than two women together. Two men will almost always want an open relationship, which is fine, but not easy to maintain in the long-term, and heterosexual couples can be so unevenly matched in their desires. Personally, I do believe in monogamy—a lot—but I also believe that, specifically for men, it goes against their very nature."

"Very biased, indeed."

"I know very well I'm over-simplifying to get my point across, but I've seen it happen over and over again."

"Purely theoretically, the argument you make is sound, but, of course, there's the small matter of attraction to take into consideration."

"True, but what are you saying, Alice? That in all of your fifty-one years, minus the years when you were a child, you have never looked at a woman and thought: hm, yum?"

"*Yum?*" I blurt it out because I feel caught out. And whereas I've certainly admired many a woman's physique, or fellow female lawyer's work ethic, or the way Kirsty Young's accent rolls off her tongue on *Crimewatch*, I've certainly never consciously entertained the notion of… of *Yum*. Not until last night at the beach, it dawns on me now. "No." I shake my head for emphasis.

"Your loss." Joy sits there grinning. "But yes, I am truly and profoundly biased, I admit."

"Have you ever been attracted to men?" I ask quickly, to deflect attention from the blush creeping up my neck.

"Not since I realised that I wasn't required to be."

I can't help but laugh, again, at Joy's quick one-liners, and her forwardness, and how she is so intensely sure of herself when it comes to this. Not that I've ever had any reason to doubt my sexuality. "Have you slept with men?" Her forwardness is surely rubbing off on me.

"Uh-uh!" Joy wags her finger at me. "Wait your turn, Alice. My question now."

I smile at Joy, a wide smile coming from a place deep within me, and for the briefest of instances, I let myself feel it. This giddiness, this sensation of being totally at ease with someone, so at ease that I'm telling her things I've never told anyone.

"So…" Joy wraps her arms around her knees a bit tighter. "I've saved the big one for last." She grins mock-apologetically. I do think she's enjoying this immensely as well, which flatters me. "Do you, Alice McAllister," she begins, her voice low and dramatic, "satisfy yourself? Your sexual needs, I mean."

I huff out a loud, nervous laugh, while shaking my head. She's crossing a line now, and the giddiness of only a few seconds ago, flees my system rapidly. Joy stares at me intently, as if not wanting to miss a split second of my reaction. "I'm sorry, Joy." To my horror, my voice is trembling a little. "I'm not going to answer that question. That is just too personal."

She scrunches her lips into a pout. "Fair enough, I guess." Her eyes are still on me. "But Alice, just so you know, your refusal to reply is a response in itself."

Why would she do this? I think. Why would she endeavour to end this perfectly fine day we've had, this companionship that has grown between us, by asking me something crass like that. I let my guard down too much. "I beg your pardon?" I push my chair back, ready to make my escape.

"Alice, I'm sorry. I went too far. It's what I do sometimes." Still in her chair, she scuttles closer to me and puts her hands on my knees. "Forgive me?"

"Feel free to make all the assumptions about me you want, Joy. If I'm an uptight old spinster in your eyes, then that's perfectly fine with me. The only thing I was after was a quiet holiday on my own. I let you crash here, put up with all your displays of, of… loose morals, and this is how you show your gratitude? By asking me the rudest questions? I don't think so." As I say the words, I know I'm exaggerating, know that I'm taking something I can't deal with out on her. I also can't move because her fingers are claws around my knees, and her touch, innocent though it is, is doing something to my skin—something I can't rationally explain.

Luckily, Joy removes her hands from my knees, and holds them up in a gesture of peace. "Okay, before we both say things we don't mean: time out."

I see this as my chance to get up. My brain hasn't been this rampant with emotion since… since as long as I can remember. I have no idea what to do with myself, what to say next, how to get myself out of this pickle.

"Please, Alice, accept my apology." Joy looks sincere when she says it but, even though her face is half-obscured, it's as though I can sense something else. It's not just forgiveness she's after, I conclude. With the corner of her mouth turned up like that, and the stare she keeps laying on me, I think she's also trying to tell me that she has sensed something. Not just that she hit on subjects I never talk about—dating, sex, masturbation—but that, perhaps, the reason why I fled the beach last night might have been something else entirely than fatigue. "I'll be a good girl from now on," she adds. "As good as you want me to be."

"Apology accepted," I say, because I don't want things to be like this between us. "Just… respect my boundaries a bit more, please."

"I will." She puts her hand over where her heart is, and gives me a tiny nod of the head. Then she extends her hand and offers it to me. "Let's shake on it." I meet her hand and take it in mine. We shake while her eyes are still fixed on mine. "And for the record, Alice, you really are a great listener. You're not nearly as uptight as I first thought you were, and I had a truly wonderful time with you today. Thank you." She's still clutching my hand in hers. I make no move to remove my hand from her grasp either. So we stand there, under the feeble light of a quarter moon, hand in hand, and something is changing within me. I just haven't figured out what.

CHAPTER SEVEN

In bed, I can't stop thinking about Joy's last question. Not the untowardness of it, or the fact that it threw me so much, but what it implies about Joy. What is she doing in her room right now? After the prolonged handshake, we both retired to our bedrooms, and ever since slipping under the sheets, it's all I can think about. As though Joy has awakened something inside me. Perhaps it all started when she first jumped into the pool with her top off.

I've already got up twice. Once to look out of the window, at that sliver of moon that has witnessed this—for now—unspeakable change within me, and once to take off my nightgown which, suddenly, seems too much. Too warm for the hot Portuguese night, and too constricting for the thoughts swirling in my brain.

And while I lie here, my mind drifting to Joy's bedroom on the other side of the wall, her last question still fresh in my mind, my naked body feels free under the flimsy sheet, and I think to myself: why not? Because Joy was right, I'm not in the habit of 'satisfying myself'. Frankly, it's not something I allow my mind to dwell on. Until she brought it up. But now that it has, I feel as though I should try. For someone who puts a lot of work in maintaining a healthy body, I spend far too little time enjoying it. So, I spread my legs. A strange sensation at first. To feel the shift of air there, between my legs. I trail one finger between my breasts, and marvel at how my skin breaks out in goosebumps. It's all about intention, I conclude. I've traced a finger over my skin many a time, but never with this in mind, and just the notion of it changes everything.

How would Joy do this? I wonder. Would she fondle her breasts first? Or go straight for where the action is? And it's thoughts like these that throw me the most. The Alice who boarded a plane to the Algarve mere days ago, would never have them. The easy conclusion would be to say this is my midlife crisis. Acute and obvious. Because here I lie in bed—and this seems most ridiculous to me—lusting after a woman twenty-two years my junior. It's not right. It's not who I am. She's Miranda's daughter, for crying out loud. But yet, it's true. It's happening. The real question is: can it be undone? Because this is preposterous.

Does this make me worse than Alan? At least his new wife is only ten years younger than he is, and he was much younger than I am now when he met her. No, this is not something I can allow. It was just a momentary lapse in judgement. I'm kind enough with myself to admit that we all display signs of weakness sometimes. It's human. I'm human. It's the circumstances, and the conversation we had, and Joy's blunt but charming way. It's a fluke. As of tomorrow, I will keep my distance. I'll stay off the alcohol. I'll discover the Algarve by myself and give Joy all the space she wants in the house, which, one day, will belong to her. It's easy enough to keep up for a few more days, and then she'll be gone, out of my life, and I'll forget about this episode, pretend it never even occurred. No one will ever know.

For this to happen, it's imperative I close my legs this instant. So, I do. Easily. I throw the sheet off me and reach for my nightgown which I draped over a chair earlier, and quickly put it on, as though it will make it so I never took it off in the first place. As though this simple act of covering up my naked body can erase the madness in my brain—or no, not my brain. Something more primal than that. My loins, yes. Anyway, bygones, I've covered myself up and I'm Alice McAllister again, a respectable woman and respected lawyer. It's all over.

I slip back under the covers, take a few deep breaths, and try to sleep.

✷ ✷ ✷

I wake up with my nightie twisted tightly around my waist, after the worst night of sleep I've had in years. I'm usually a good sleeper, because I make a point of being at peace with myself before I go to bed, and I maintain excellent sleep etiquette. Keeping last night's feelings at bay may require a bit more effort, but I'm more than prepared to make as much effort as needed. To become myself again. Before I get up, I reach for the guidebook on my night stand, and choose my destination for the day. I want to be prepared when I run into Joy, want to have my words ready to speak —to clearly state my intentions.

I read something about Vila Real de Santo António, which is close to the border with Spain and will keep me out of the house for most part of the day. Perfect. Culture, pretty landscapes and redemption.

In the shower, I hum, pleased with myself and how I'm handling the situation. Relieved, even, to not have to deal with whatever was stirring within me. And happy to have found the means to lock it away.

Ideally, Joy will still be in bed, so I can just leave her a note and have breakfast en route. I'm hopeful, because she did drink a lot yesterday, and a hangover is a real possibility. The first moment of deflation comes when I walk past her bedroom door and find it open. But I can deal with this. It's not even a setback, just a situation a fraction less than ideal.

"Morning." Joy is in the kitchen making coffee. She turns to me when she hears me, and she's wearing that barely-there tank top again and, truthfully, it makes me swallow hard for a second. But what it also does is spur me on to leave as soon as possible. "Just in time. I'm making coffee. Want some?" Joy lets her gaze travel across my body. "You're all tarted up this morning. Fancy date?" She laughs that carefree—and, come to think of it, rather inconsiderate —laugh of hers.

"I've decided to take a day trip to Vila Real de Santo António," I declare formally.

"Oh." There's no hint of disappointment in her voice. "Do you want to be alone or would you like me to join you?"

"I would like to take the day for myself, if you don't mind." My words sound as practiced as they are. Before I opened the door of my room earlier, I was pacing in the exact way I do when I'm preparing for a big client meeting.

"Sure." Joy crosses her arms over her chest. "Does this have anything to do with last night? I mean, you didn't mention this day trip at all yesterday, so I'm just wondering."

Another question I had prepared for. Human beings are so predictable, really. "Nothing at all. I just want to make the most of my time here. And this way, you can have the house to yourself today. Fully relax."

"I'm quite relaxed already, Alice, but all right." Joy doesn't move, just stands there, looking at me sceptically. "How about I make us dinner then? Give me a call when you're about an hour away, and I'll have it ready."

"That won't be necessary. I expect to be back rather late."

She cocks her head now. "Okay. Very well. I shan't wait up for you then." She imitates my unnatural tone of voice. "Have fun."

I ignore the way she's speaking to me. "Thank you. You too."

I walk past her, to the front door, and leave.

★ ★ ★

At first, in the car, I wish I had Bruce Springsteen albums to listen to, but then, on second thought, I'm glad I haven't because they would only make me think of that near-perfect day we spent yesterday. And about the odds of a girl like Joy enjoying music made when she was barely born. I like old things, she said, which sounds so disrespectful now.

On the drive over, when my thoughts are scattered and free-flowing, I applaud myself on the good decision I made. On how I handled this maturely. But by the time I arrive at Vila Real de Santo António, when the blue of the sky floors me again, I'm reminded why I hardly ever travel: because, more than any other activity, doing it alone makes me feel disproportionally lonely. Then I start missing Joy's easy chatter of the day before, and how she spoke about her father, and the chat we had in the car. And I don't know how it's possible, but I realise that I miss her company. It's not logical, it's not sane, it's hardly proper, but it's how it is.

I've only been en route back a few minutes before I pull over and take my phone out of my purse. It's an old-fashioned non-smart model, because I draw the line somewhere, and I know it would impair my sanity if I carried work emails around with me everywhere I went. I put Joy's number in my phone after Miranda gave it to me when she called that first day I was here, for emergencies.

This is not a change of heart, I say to myself. But as I felt increasingly miserable in the course of the afternoon, I was able to convince myself very easily that, if I truly wanted to put this behind me, escaping Joy's proximity was not the best method. I had to tackle it head-on: by chasing the unwanted images from my mind while face-to-face with her.

I compose a text, erase it, write the exact same words again, then send it.

I'll be back by 7 if you still want to have dinner with me.

A little needy, perhaps. And a tad passive-aggressive. All adjectives that have never applied to me before. On the long drive back, with nothing but silence in the car, I know that I'm fooling myself. "Nice try," I tell myself—my silly, wanton, overly eager self. Because what has transpired in my psyche over the past three days, subtle at first, but then bursting to the fore with great explosions of realisation, cannot be undone. Not even I, with my stiff upper lip, my carefully planned out days, and my emotions in check, can undo what Joy has unleashed in me. It's only normal that I'm terrified, and my actions are stuttering cries for something. I just don't know what it is exactly. I certainly haven't turned lesbian overnight. I don't know much, but I know that. I also know that I want to spend more time with Joy. The desire beats in my blood like a gentle, steady drum. Being with her brings out a different side of me. A side I like. She makes me more communicative, more in touch with my emotions, more ready to share. More alive.

My phone is on the passenger seat, and I glance at it furtively, waiting for a reply. She's probably in the pool, I think. Most likely with nothing on at all. The thought causes me to have a hot flash and I turn up the air-conditioning. Then my phone makes its old-fashioned beep, and I pull over again.

Sure thing, the message reads. That's it. And her curt reply makes me wonder again, makes me question my sanity. But it's not as though I'm speeding back to Quinta do Lago for something unseemly. It's a meal. It's company. A new friend. As unlikely a pair as we might be, if the past few days have convinced me of anything, it's that Joy and I could be friends. After all, I've been friends with her mother for the longest time, and her father was a good friend too, before he passed away. She's quite different from the both of them, but reflections come through. Miranda's zany zest for life, her taste for luxury, for unashamedly taking what belongs to her. And Paul's—although this is harder to remember—directness, his stout unwillingness to care one iota about what anyone thought about him. Joy Perkins is a child of her parents, for sure, but she's also, and even more so, her own person. A funny, relaxed, slightly arrogant girl with her heart in the right place. A young woman still looking for her place in the world. Much the opposite of me, but isn't that something to value in a friend? A different take on things.

The option to look at an issue from a totally different perspective and just step out of my own head, the one I've been in my entire life.

CHAPTER EIGHT

"Friends?" I say, as soon as I walk into the door of the house.

"Of course," Joy replies. She's in the kitchen and, to my huge surprise, she's wearing a bra. Oddly—or not—it's the first thing I notice. The black straps peeking from underneath her tank top. "Good day?"

"Not too bad." I feel it squirming inside me already, this beast, this presence, this announcement of change.

"Feel free to have a swim. I'm making grilled chicken and it needs a bit longer. There's sangria in the fridge, if you would like to partake."

"What a feast." I'm still standing near the door, as though ready to make a swift escape.

"I aim to please." Joy plants her hands on the kitchen counter behind her, making her chest jut out. "Why don't you come in, Alice? I'm not going to bite." She does that giggle, the slightly offensive one. Only Joy has the uncanny ability to offend and charm me at the same time. Or perhaps, it now dawns on me, it's called flirting.

"No need to dress up, okay?"

"You've certainly dressed up." I make a point of staring at her chest, in spite of how dizzy it makes me feel.

"Yeah, I went to the market in Loulé, and I figured I had to cage the girls. Not to worry, though, that bra is coming off asap."

"As if I would worry about that." I make my way to the corridor, but don't turn the corner before shooting her a wink.

★ ★ ★

Of course, she has made the sangria very strong—I doubt someone like Joy would even realise it doesn't need *that* much alcohol. I opt to sit in the shade and take small sips, carefully measuring the time in between drinking, so as not to let it get to my head too much. The last thing I need to be this evening is tipsy, but I don't want to be rude, either.

"I'm going for a quick dip," Joy says as she saunters out of the house. "Let me know when the oven beeps."

Perhaps out of courtesy, she's wearing the hot pink bikini top. I'm at a point where I see messages in everything, and I'm not as good an expert in non-verbal communication as I ought to be.

"It'll come with experience," Miranda used to say. But it never really did. Miranda, my once mentor, who took me under her wing after I had just finished university and started as a trainee at Beechums. Miranda, whom I got along with so well, that it was a no-brainer to start our own law firm after five years of working together.

"Sure," I say to Joy, and when she cocks her head like that, I see a bit of Miranda in the lift of her cheekbones, and in that demanding, unwavering stare.

"You're really not coming in? It's illegal to not go in the pool at least once a day when you're staying at this house, you know?" Her stance is all bravado, like she's testing me. One hand on her jutted-out hips, her lips scrunched into that half-pout she does so well.

"I'm a lawyer, Joy," I say. "I believe I know my rights."

"Suit yourself." She turns and, without any hesitation, dives in.

Even though, despite the shower I just took, my skin is overheated and sweat puddles in the small of my back, I'm wise enough to avoid a situation where I would find myself in the pool with Joy. Additionally, I don't enjoy having dinner while dripping wet. It's not right.

I sip my drink as I watch Joy, who swims a few quick

laps. Her phone is on the table and it keeps lighting up with messages. If it were waterproof, I'm sure she'd take it into the pool with her.

I have nothing else to do but watch how Joy pushes herself out of the pool. She doesn't use the built-in steps, but prefers to hoist herself up on her arms, her biceps gleaming with water, and bring her feet in between her legs. Her movement makes me realise, again, how much younger she is than me. She towels off with her back to me, then pulls her hair into a high pony tail.

"Bear with me, Alice," she says. "I messed up the timing a bit, but it should be ready now." On her way in, she grabs her phone, her eyes immediately trained on its tiny screen. I hear her sigh, then patter farther into the house.

"My dad taught me how to make this when I was twelve years old," she says, as she deposits a tray onto the table. "In this very kitchen."

The chicken is golden-brown, its skin deliciously crispy.

"I hope you don't mind a bit of spice. Over the years, I've added more and more piri-piri." She flashes me a grin before taking a large gulp of sangria.

"This is truly scrumptious," I say, although my tastebuds do need to adjust to the heat of the spices.

"Let's enjoy it in memory of Paul Perkins—" She gets cut off by the sound of another message arriving on her phone. "You know what? I'm just going to turn this off. Someone is massively getting on my tits."

I raise an eyebrow, more amused by the expression she uses than curious about who keeps messaging her.

"It's Alex. She's drunk texting me." Joy shuts down her phone demonstratively.

"Oh." I put down my fork. "Does she want you back?" It's more a joke. An indulgence I allow myself in the form of a quick, easy question.

"Who knows what Alex really wants." Joy pushes her phone to the very end of the table. "Either way, I'm no longer interested. Tell me about your day, Alice."

I don't tell her about how, long before I was supposed to start making my way back, the prospect of seeing her at the house pulled me towards it. Nor do I let her know how much I missed her company in the car. Instead, I marvel at the delights of Vila Real de Santo António, and the beauty of this region, and how uninterrupted days of nothing but blue skies above you must be the best cure for just about everything.

"I'm glad you had a good time," she says as we reach the end of our meal. "This morning, it really seemed as though you were running away from me. I'm making a point of being more respectful towards you now. I hope you've noticed."

"I have." So that's why she put on that bikini top earlier. "And I did, uh, sort of run away from you."

"We had a moment, didn't we?" Joy has pushed her plate away and sits back watching me. "Last night before we went to bed. I got the distinct impression you were more upset about that than about what I asked you."

"I'm not sure what you mean by having a moment." I'm glad Joy waited until the meal was over to corner me like this. Is this what she means by being more respectful? Or am I being too uptight again?

"Can I speak freely? If you were anyone else, I wouldn't ask, but I don't want you to clam up on me again. If you don't want to have this conversation, we won't. But, and perhaps you're not even fully aware of it, Alice, I think you do. I even think you *need* to have it."

I mull over the day I've had, and my mind drifts back to 'the moment' she's referring to, and I know I'm deliberately playing dumb about it, and it really doesn't suit a woman my age. "Okay. Be my guest."

But Joy doesn't say anything. Is it her way of making *me* say something? More sweat drips down my spine. I'm just about to utter something deflecting, when she gets up out of her chair and heads towards me. Flabbergasted, but with my stomach turning in on itself with unprecedented excitement, I witness how she plants her hands on the armrests of my chair, leans in, and kisses me full on the lips.

That's speaking very freely, I think, at first, because my mind is racing, and so is my pulse and—what is happening? I push myself forwards, though, in order to better receive her kiss, and when I feel her lips open a fraction, I do the same, and then our tongues meet, and it's as though I can feel it in the tiniest cells in my body. I feel it tingle in my toes, and chase up my spine—where, oddly, the sweat has cooled—and ripple underneath my skin.

Joy brings her hands to my cheeks, her fingers splayed, and the gesture engulfs me in another shockwave of emotion, and desire, and abandon. Her tongue twirls freely in my mouth now, meeting mine, darting to and fro, and all of this is, by far, the strangest thing to have happened to me in decades. I barely remember kissing a man, yet I know this is distinctly different. It's softer, gentler, endlessly more erotic.

And even though I'm really still too stunned to move, I bring my own hands to Joy's neck, and I pull her closer, because where she is right now, is exactly where I want her to be. We kiss for long, slow, delicious minutes, which are probably only seconds, but time stretches into infinity as I surrender, as I let go of everything, and recognise wholeheartedly what it is I felt on the beach two nights ago.

Desire.

When, at last, we break from our lip-lock, and my brain starts working again, I immediately feel myself stiffen. Because what does this mean? Does this make me gay? And where will this go?

"Fuck, Alice," Joy pants. "I've been wanting to do that for a while."

"You have?" I ask, stupidly.

Joy just smiles and leans in again, but I can't enjoy this

second kiss as much as the first. I'm no longer stunned into shock, but into something else: realisation. When the kiss ends, and Joy looks at me with what I think is longing in her eyes, I can't help but back off a bit.

"Do you want me to stop?" She hovers over me, her breasts level with my eyes, and I don't know what to say or do.

"I, uh, just thought you wanted to talk," I mumble.

She grins, and sits down, putting her hands on my knees. "Sometimes it's easier to say something without words."

I wish I could go home and think this over. Give it the analytic Alice treatment I give my clients. But I'm trapped in this house with Joy, who is making me feels things I can't name, I can't even fathom.

"When did you want to kiss me?" I ask.

She pulls her face into a quizzical expression, as though contemplating my question vigorously. "When we were at the beach. I was so disappointed when you left." She catches my ankle in between hers. "And last night. Definitely last night. God, I was flirting so heavily with you. And you were responding so… favourably. Until I got impatient and screwed up."

"Look, uh, Joy, I'm not saying I didn't enjoy that kiss, but this is extremely confusing for me."

"I understand that. It's quite confusing for me as well." She squeezes her fingers a bit harder around my knees. "But, please, do me one favour, Alice. Please, don't go into hiding in your room. Please, don't leave me here by myself to process this."

Truth be told, it is my first instinct. I need to mull this over. At least attempt to explain it, and give it a place in my life. "I won't," I say instead.

"In the end it's only a kiss. It doesn't need to be any more than that if that's what you want."

"I have absolutely no clue as to what I want." I

interlace my fingers behind my neck and let my head fall back.

"*I* do." Her fingers creep up my thighs just a tiny bit, but enough to nearly make me jump out of my chair. "I'm sorry." She removes her hands entirely from my body, and releases my ankle from the prison of her clasped-together legs. "I have a tendency to get way ahead of myself."

"I won't claim to know what it is you want from me right now, although I do have an inkling, but a kiss is absolutely definitely as far as this can go for me."

"Absolutely *and* definitely, huh?" Joy leans back in her chair. "Of course."

"And, no matter what happens, you can never tell anyone about this."

"Cross my heart."

My heartbeat slows, and the most acute rigidness is leaving my muscles. I'm starting to recover from the kiss, starting to feel a little like myself again—even though I have no idea who that is anymore.

"Do you want to talk?" she asks.

"Freely, you mean?" This time, *I* stretch my legs, and lightly touch my shin to hers, so she knows that, despite not fully realising it until it occurred, I have thought of kissing her as well.

Joy giggles, then bites her bottom lip. "Well, Alice, if this is what happens when I keep my top on—and wear a bra when you come home—I do wonder where it will end once I fully dress up."

I'm so grateful for how she defuses the tension, and her comment coaxes a laugh from me that is more than a nervous chuckle. And then, I want to kiss her again. So much so, in fact, that I'm the one rising from my chair, towering over her, and pressing my lips to hers. Instantly, her hands are in my hair, drawing me closer. And, this time, our mouths open at once, letting each other in, and I feel like I'm floating on air, like decades of ignoring the urge to be touched are being erased, dumped into oblivion without mercy, because as of now, I *do* want to be touched. Oh, I do.

Meanwhile, night is falling, and a brooding darkness surrounds us. I'm torn, because in this moment, I want more, but I can't be sure until I let the moment pass. Until I can make my own informed decision.

"How about a swim?" I say, more as a means of protecting myself than out of a desire to be in the water—although I could use the cooling off.

"You're full of surprises," Joy replies. I straighten my back and she glares at me from under her lashes. What is this to her? Some holiday fun? A rebound thing? A string in her bow? She gets up and plants her hands on my sides. "May I?" she asks, and starts lifting my top.

I shake my head, and cover her hands with mine, holding them in place. "I'm going to put on my bathing suit." I need a moment to myself, to check myself in the mirror and see if my face is the same. "I'll be right back." I stare into her eyes briefly before pecking her gently on the cheek.

She nods, and I head inside.

When I'm in my room, I lean against the closed door for a few seconds. I just kissed Miranda's twenty-nine-year-old daughter. The mere thought of it is too much to just sit with on my own in my room. The urge to go back out there, to just be in Joy's presence and experience this with her, overwhelms me.

I quickly disrobe and, feeling more daring than possibly ever in my life, I put on my brand new—and never worn—bikini instead of my tried and tested one-piece bathing suit. I check myself in the mirror before I leave the room, but I can barely stand to look at myself. *You're processing*, I tell myself. *It's normal.*

Joy doesn't say anything when I emerge from my room. She sits on the steps of the pool. She hasn't taken her top off and, for once, I don't know how I feel about that. Her smile says it all, though. As if not opting for the one-piece is a clear gesture on my part. I guess it is.

As soon as I'm in the pool, I throw my head back, covering my ears under water, which gives me that suspended sensation of not being anywhere at all, of floating somewhere no one has any influence over me—it's just my body drifting, blackness pierced only by a few stars above me, my weight carried by the water.

A pair of hands touches my back, brings me out of it. But, because I know it's Joy, I let myself float for a while longer, until it dawns on me that this is giving her ample opportunity to scan the parts of my body that float above the water's surface. Self-conscious, I lower my legs until I stand. She might have mentioned that I'm in good shape, and I do take excellent care of my body, but signs of ageing are inevitable. Not something I would usually have a problem with—it's only nature taking its course—but next to Joy's unmistakably youthful appearance, I suddenly do have an issue. It's the contrast, and what is says about me. Although it's not Joy's youth I'm attracted to first and foremost—not that it doesn't play a part. How can such an essential characteristic of hers not? It's who she is, and how she has guided me to this moment. It's what she has done to me.

"I'm not a shy maiden," Joy says. "I'm perfectly happy to respect your wishes, and I'm pretty good at reading people, but when I want someone, I go for it." She takes a step closer, into the most sensual live image I've ever seen. Drops of water rain down from her hair over her face, as though licking and kissing her where I want to. "I've shown you *and* I've told you. Your move."

My move? Is this a seduction manoeuvre? More flirting? A way to coax me out of my shell? It feels like, ever since Joy arrived, I've been transported to another planet—or another galaxy altogether. One where my rules, the ones I've lived by my entire life, are tested and, mostly rejected afterwards. But I try not to look at the situation from the outside, try not to analyse. Try to simply enjoy the moment. My resolve that this could 'absolutely and definitely' not go any further tonight, seems to be crumbling ridiculously easily. But, just so I can't claim later to have lost control over my common sense, I do check in with myself. Do I want this? Do I want to make my move? All I get back from myself is a slow pulse in an undefined place, but, really, if I'm honest, right between my legs—where I was afraid to touch myself last night. Maybe tonight is our night. Why wait? What purpose can it possibly serve? I want Joy. I feel it tingle on my skin, feel it in the pucker of my lips, feel it in the sway of my hips—rocking towards her.

Under water, I find her hands, and pull her close. We kiss under the moonlight.

CHAPTER NINE

Putting on my bikini was a big waste of time, because now, I can't wait to get it off. It's a struggle because it's wet, but I refuse to lie on the bed with it while it's still moist. We kissed our way out of the pool and through the open French windows of my room. Hands only groping for neck and hair, so far. I feel like a switch has been flipped, like my armour is coming down at an exponentially fast pace, like years—decades—of my life need to be caught up on in one night. I really don't have a clue, even though I am a woman, just like Joy, and I do know how it works, but I'm insecure, and I really need her to be that not-shy person she claims to be. There's no doubt in my mind she will easily comply with that wish. It's what makes her extra irresistible. And I don't think about tomorrow, or any time after now. And, perhaps, in this moment, I am who I was always supposed to be. Touched, desired, a woman come alive.

My top comes off and we break from yet another frantic lip-lock—they've grown more urgent as time has progressed—so that I can throw it to the ground, and not care about how reckless and unusual that is for me. Joy smiles, but it's a different smile than the ones I've been greeted with so far: there is lust in there, so undeniable, my pulse quickens even more, and I feel my heart throw itself against my ribcage as if it's screaming, 'Oh yes. Now. Oh yes.'

To be able to do this, I can't be allowed any more time to reflect. I need my heart to behave like that, and my loins to feel as if they're going crazy, to feel they might explode if they remain untouched tonight. I feel my nipples stiffen further at the exposure to the air. Joy is taking her top off and, although it's nothing I haven't seen before, it's different now. It's foreplay. Not implied, not hidden, not a cocky flirt. It's real. She's coming for me, and for the first time our bare breasts touch, and it's enough to elicit a low groan from my throat.

"What are you doing to me?" I whisper. A silly question, but poignant enough to make her eyes glaze over with an extra layer of lust, and the sight makes me go weak at the knees.

I have never done this, I think. And it applies to so many factors. I've never had sex with anyone who wasn't my spouse or my fiancé. I've never slept with anyone out of pure lust, and lust alone. I've never touched a woman this way. I've never, ever, been this utterly turned on. So turned on, in fact, I want to tear my bikini bottoms off me, and do the same to Joy. To just fully give in to this madness. I might as well.

So, I do. I let my finger trail down Joy's spine, along her side, and then briefly slip into the waistband of her bikini bottoms. It's hardly tearing off, but it's close enough for me.

"I knew it," Joy huffs. "Fuck, I knew it."

I have no idea what she means by that, and I don't want to ruin the moment by asking, so I make a mental note to question her later—although chances are I will surely have forgotten by then.

She starts pushing her bikini down, squirming against me, and I take the opportunity to do the same to mine, but this suddenly strikes me as too bold a move, too far removed from something I would do, so I stop and wait for Joy to do it. As if she knows, and we're existing on entirely the same wavelength, after she's got rid of hers, she traces a finger over my lower belly, on the skin above my bikini.

"I'll take care of everything, Alice," she says. And I believe her. Her finger wanders down, exploring the wet fabric slowly, giving my body time to adjust to her touch. She presses her lips to mine again, leaving a gap between our bodies so her finger can meander farther down. It's so close to the centre of the most violent throbbing in my body, that I'm fearful of what may happen when her finger glides over. Then it does, and my breath stutters, and my knees buckle, but, most of all, a warmth spreads inside me, like butterflies waking up aglow with light.

"Good God," I moan. What I actually want to say is, 'Take them off. Please.' And this, too, Joy understands, because soon both her hands are tugging my bikini bottoms over my behind. She crouches down to slide them over my legs, and the sight of her down there, while I'm completely naked, ignites another round of violent throbbing.

Whereas I had expected to grow more self-conscious the less clothes I wore, the opposite is true. A boldness settles in my core. I want to spread my legs for her. Want her to touch me and lick me—years of suppressed lust are catching up with me.

"Let's get into bed," Joy says when we're face-to-face again. "Lie on your back."

I enjoy being told exactly what to do. It's a safety in this brand new world I find myself in. It brings a sense of security I need for this sort of abandon.

Once we're both lying down, I on my back, she on her side next to me, she smiles. No words are required. With two fingers, she traces the line of my jaw, my throat, the hollow of my neck, the cleft between my breasts. Then, her fingers curve beneath my breast to move upward, up the swell of it, towards my nipple, where they begin another circle. Joy repeats this pattern a few times, until my nipple is, quite surely, the hardest it has ever been. She leans forwards a bit, and I expect her to kiss me, but instead she brings her lips to my nipple. And everything she does is done with such gentleness, such care, such intent, that, instinctively, my legs go wide. While Joy sucks my puckered nipple into her mouth, I enjoy the free flow of air between my legs, the intimacy of touch, and how it makes my ever-churning mind stop worrying.

After she lets my nipple slip from her lips, leaving it wet and wanting more, she shuffles upwards a bit, and looks into my eyes. "You're such a beautiful woman," she says, and I can tell that she means it. That she's not just saying it to get something from me, or to flatter me. Or to get me into bed with her, because I already am. "Do you want me to tell you what I'm going to do to you, or just do it?" Her solemn smile curves into a wicked grin.

"Surprise me," I say.

"Oh, I will." She brings her hand to my throat, slips it behind my neck, and kisses me again. I melt into this kiss more than into the ones that came before, because this is it. It feels like my first time all over again—though I have absolutely no recollection of my actual first time. All I remember is that it was with Alan. That's it.

The kiss grows fiercer, and she catches my bottom lip between her teeth and gives it a slight tug and, again, I feel it everywhere. Parts of me awaken, long dormant body parts that, like in a fairy tale, could only be woken up by a kiss from the right person.

Joy hoists herself on top of me and straddles me. I can feel her pubic hair tickle my belly, but more than that, it's as though I can *feel* her eyes on me. The swoop of her gaze flicking over my breasts, my face, focusing on my lips. Is she considering what she'll do next? Judging from the look in her eyes and the slant of her neck, and the absolute self-assuredness she displays, it will be nothing short of spectacular. Although, this night, for me, is already nothing short of spectacular. No matter what happens next, come tomorrow I will be a different woman.

Joy lowers her torso and takes my other nipple in her mouth. Her own nipples poke into my skin, and I can feel how hard they are, but I resist the urge to bring my hands in between us and touch them. Instead, I bring my hands to her hair, twirl my fingers around a few strands. My hands follow her head downwards as she scoots lower, not breaking contact between her lips and my skin. She licks a moist path around my belly button, and the tension within me rises again. I'm not sure how much more it can rise before the lid comes off. The entire expanse of my skin has turned into gooseflesh, the smallest patch of it hyper-sensitised. And then, her mouth reaches my pubic hair, and she lifts herself off me, because with her downwards movement, my legs have closed—and neither one of us is happy with that, I gather.

She doesn't need to tell me to spread them. I do so happily, fully conscious, very aware of what I'm doing and what I'm becoming. She positions herself between my legs, and she just looks. Maybe she's suddenly aware of the fact that what she's about to do hasn't been done in a very long time, and she does have a reverent side to her personality, though I doubt it. Maybe it's just what she does—because her gaze on my sex doesn't miss its effect. She might as well be stroking me there instead of just looking at me, that's how I'm pulsing down there, and wanting, and getting oh so wet.

Then, she cuts her eyes at me, locks them on mine. "I'm going to lick your pussy, Alice." She lets her tongue dart out of her mouth, flick along her lips—like the cat who got the cream.

Me, I can't smile, can barely acknowledge what she says, I can only groan, because I want it so badly by then. Want her lips on me so feverishly. And then, they are. She kisses my nether lips—my pussy, as she called it—and I go liquid. This is more than a switch being flipped. This is like a machine being rebooted after years of non-service. Like an engine roaring to life after too many years of being discarded. She kisses her way upwards, to my clitoris, to where I was reluctant to touch myself the night before. Oh, how much can change in twenty-four hours.

I reaffirm the position of my hands in her hair, because I need to touch her, need that connection to the person who is doing this to me—who is undoing me. Her tongue slides along my most intimate parts now, like a paint brush which can, just with a few expert strokes, produce a perfect image that wasn't there before. And the image I'm seeing is me without my overly long skirts, and blouses buttoned up to the top, and my always proper behaviour, be it with clients or with friends. It's me in all my naked glory, bursting into a life I had forgotten about, at the tongue of another woman.

Joy's tongue flicks and flicks, and I pant and pant. I squirm against the mattress, no doubt unhooking the sheets, and I press my thighs against Joy's ears and pull at her hair because, apparently, that is the kind of person I am in bed. Who knew?

And then, just as I'm about to lose it, to give into to that roller coaster thundering through my flesh, that pinnacle of pleasure she's been building towards, I feel a finger entering me. And it's too much.

"Aaah," I cry out, and I surprise myself with the sound of my own voice, because it sounds like someone else entirely. It sounds like the new me. Joy's finger touches me, and her tongue keeps swirling stubbornly, and then I surrender. I surrender to Joy and give her everything I have and, with it, shed the image of the old Alice, and become me, at last.

Once my muscles relax, I find myself clutching my head in my hands. I am so utterly shocked that all I can say is "Good God." And then I cry a little bit, not just out of delight, but also because of what I've allowed myself to miss out on. Years of this. Years of tenderness, and just pure fun and pleasure.

Joy has crawled upwards and pries my hands away from my face. "Hey," she says, before kissing me on the nose. "I've barely started and you're already falling to pieces."

"What have you done to me?" I repeat the question I asked her earlier, and that went unanswered, even though I know no valid response will emerge this time either. What she has done to me can't be put into words even if we tried.

"I told you what I was going to do. I licked your pussy." There's something about how she says the word pussy. It must be because she lived in the US for so long. Maybe it's a common term there, but it's certainly not part of my vocabulary.

"My pussy." I say the word slowly, as if trying it out. It sounds so crass and at the same time so terribly exciting.

"It's magnificent," Joy says, while leaning the side of her head on an upturned palm. "As are you."

"Well, you *are* a self-proclaimed cougar lover. You can't get more cougar-y than me."

"I'm definitely pushing the limit with you, that's for sure." She smiles when she says it. A broad, satisfied smile. "I meant what I said though. I was only just getting started."

And as much as I want her to keep exploring me, and coaxing more and more pleasure from me, I want to feel her body give itself that way at my hands. "Yes, well, the cougar is hungry and needs to be fed." I can barely believe the words that come from my mouth.

"Oh, Alice." Joy gives a throaty laugh while running her fingertips over my torso. "You're not going to fight me for top already, are you?"

"Sorry?" Once again, I have no idea what she means.

She chuckles some more. "Don't worry, I'll explain later."

I shift to my side a little, to be able to fully face her. "I want you, Joy. Is that okay?"

"More than okay." She kisses me again and she tastes of sangria and chlorine from the pool and, I guess, of me. "Have your way with me."

Her last sentence fazes me. Do I just repeat what she did to me? Or follow my instincts? What does she like? Will

I know? So many questions. Too many for this moment, which should be one of exhilaration, and slight bemusement, but mostly of arousal and the desire to please her. So, instead of allowing more questions to enter my mind, I focus on Joy's smiling face, and on the prospect of finally touching those breasts with which she has taunted me for days.

I push myself all the way up, until I sit next to Joy, who is now glaring at me from below, and she is truly gorgeous, with her big brown, dramatic eyes, her expressive, thick eyebrows, and that smile that can say so much. I feel as though I've become an expert in her smile over the past few days. I've seen so many versions of it. The cheeky kind. The seductive kind. The challenging kind. Now, her smile is a combination of desire, accented by that mischievous glint in her eyes, and, perhaps, apprehension—or perhaps that's just me projecting. I push any fear I might have—and I have quite a lot—to the recesses of my brain, and bow down to kiss her. I could kiss her for days. She surprised me with that kiss earlier, totally came out of left field with it, and look at us now. Is this a girl who always gets what she wants? From where I'm sitting, it definitely looks like it. We've had a few conversations, but I can hardly claim to know her, yet I'm about to… what should I call it? I honestly have no idea. I have so much to ask her, but first things first.

While we're kissing, I press her body down with mine. She clasps her hands around my neck, pulls me closer, as though she can never get enough of me, and that feeling, that sensation of being wanted, is one of the most exquisite I've ever experienced. It turns me on more than anything else. I kiss her mouth one last time and then hover my lips over her neck, inhaling her, revelling in being so close to another person, in what it does to me.

"Oh, Alice," she says, again. It's not a pleading tone she uses, but a beguiled one. "Oh, Alice, fuck me."

Another crass word that's made its way from the States,

I guess, but again, it sounds strangely enthralling coming from her lips. Daring, and a little bit dirty. Untoward, perhaps, but in a thrilling way. So that's what I'm about to do: fuck her. Last night, I heard her use the term quite loosely as well, when she was referencing my ex-husband. I took no offence then, and I take none now.

When I try to make my way down with my head the way she did earlier, she grabs me by the chin, and says, "I know you want to lick my pussy, Alice, and you can, later. I just really want you to look at me when you fuck me, I really get off on that."

I do a double-take. So much communication, so eloquently making her wishes known. In my world, and back in the day before I became sexually inactive, it was—as far as I know, and admittedly, I don't know much—unheard of, especially for a woman. But there are two women in this bed, and that changes everything.

I'm also glad for the instructions, because I want to make her feel the way she did with me earlier. And I don't mind looking at her face at all at the moment of complete surrender. It's a thrill, in fact. Something I can't wait for to happen.

As requested, I gaze into her eyes, while my hand travels along her breasts, although I have to look away when my fingers find her nipple, and squeeze it gently. And if I'm not going to taste her down there—just yet—then I at least need a taste of her nipple, of something of her. Her breasts are still so firm, their skin so supple and taut. They're tanned a golden-brown from all the topless sunbathing she's been doing, and they take my breath away.

When I wrap my lips around one of her nipples, heat rises from within me again, it travels through me in broad, unrelenting swoops. And the prospect of having the entire night, and the next two days, in fact, completely to ourselves, thrills me even more. It's an unimaginable luxury. A culmination of events. The sweetest coincidence ever. And to think I didn't want her here to begin with.

My hand focuses on her other breast, rolling her nipple between my fingers while I keep sucking on the other one. And to hold her breast in my hand like that, is already such an act of intimacy, of implied trust, of so much more than two virtual strangers who ended up sharing a holiday home. And the question repeats itself in my mind: what has she done to me?

"Oh, please, Alice," Joy moans. "You're driving me crazy."

I let her nipple slip from my lips and look at her. Her mouth is slightly agape, and in her glance I see the exquisite pain of desire unmet.

"I've had days of foreplay. I need you to fuck me now." Is this still being eloquent, or is she being downright bossy? Oh, we do indeed have so much to talk about later. And then, she has the audacity to take my hand that is resting on her breast, while I'm still a little flabbergasted, and push it down between her legs.

I can't help but smile at the sheer boldness of this girl. But it's not as if she hadn't warned me earlier: when she wants something, she goes for it. She's making swift progress, then. And, I must admit, her forthrightness turns me on, because it's a display of how I am decidedly not.

While my hand is there, I may as well venture down a bit more. I'm a little bit miffed that I can't see exactly what I'm doing, but then I think it hardly matters. My fingers skate down, through a wetness that astounds me as much as it turns me on. Who knew there could be so much raw power, so much lust hidden in a mere touch?

As though set free, and suddenly imparted with the kind of knowledge this moment requires, I circle my finger around her clitoris. Lightly at first, in wide circles, while I look into her eyes as instructed, and this too, turns me on again beyond belief. *So this is what it's supposed to be like*, I think. A level of arousal that just takes you there over and over again.

"Please, fuck me." Joy almost mouths it, so quiet are her words. I take it she wants me to push a finger inside her. And I like how the prospect of it has made her go all silent, and how her eyes go wide when my finger finds her entrance and I, slowly, slowly, enter her. But my own amazement is much greater than anything displayed on Joy's face. To be inside another woman like this, to be a part of her, to feel her warmth, is more than sensational—it's world-altering. I'm not a heavy drinker, and I've never done drugs, but as I move my finger inside Joy, I conclude this is what it must feel like. Like something you can't help but return to, something so intoxicating you will always need more of it, something so bewildering, so out of the ordinary, it can, truly, only be described as life-changing. And I'm grateful that she made me look at her face, that we can share this moment.

Joy starts bucking her hips upwards, meeting my strokes. "More," she says, her voice a low groan. "Oh, fuck, Alice." And the way she keeps repeating my name is like being brought more into the situation, like her letting me know I'm not interchangeable in this equation. This is Joy and Alice in bed together.

I slip a second finger inside her, and feel the rim of her sex contract around me. I quicken my pace, curling my fingers inside her, and the look in her eyes is one of complete focus, of determination, of stubbornness making way for the opposite of it.

When Joy comes, I feel as though I'm coming with her. We are connected not only by my fingers inside her, but also by our locked gazes, and an intimacy so intense, it shakes me to my core.

"Oh fuck," she mutters, and lets her arms fall on the pillow next to her head, as though in a gesture of capitulation. "Oh fuck, how I needed that." Unlike me, she doesn't shed a tear, but giggles instead. "Oh, Alice, come here." She throws her arms around my neck and pulls my face into her, buries her nose in my hair. "Oh, sweet Jesus, hallelujah." She giggles more, and it's infectious, although I'm also chuckling to hide how overwhelmed I am, and, ultimately, how intensely satisfied.

CHAPTER TEN

I'm awake well before dawn breaks and I lie stiffly in bed, unable to move, Joy's body glued to mine. Did this really happen? I overlook the evidence of what happened last night from the corner of my eye. Did I drink that much? But it's not the fact that I find myself waking up next to Joy that shocks me the most. It's the memory of how she made me feel. Like someone else—someone I'm definitely not. A wanton woman. A loose woman. A woman capable of sleeping with her best friend's daughter. But by God, what Joy did to me was glorious and, more than anything, I find myself wondering how I can ever return to the life I led before.

Nevertheless, I see the madness in what happened. The complete unacceptability of it. I frantically push any thought of Miranda from my mind.

Next to me, Joy sighs in her sleep, and topples onto her back. I vividly recall the rush with which I drove back from Vila Real de Santo António, that unquestionable, firm desire to be with her. I try to remember if, while I was driving back with nothing but thoughts of Joy in my head, I wanted her to kiss me—and do all the other things she did to me. And then a bigger question starts rearing its head: do I have feelings for Joy?

I must have. Or perhaps this is what is called a holiday fling. A temporary loss of my faculties, induced by too much sun and leisure time. Is this what happens to me when I stop working for a few days? I turn into—what did Joy call me?— a cougar? I can't help it. A chuckle escapes me. Alice

'Cougar' McAllister. And while renewed desire is already warming up my veins, a desire I don't plan to ignore as long as I'm on Portuguese soil, I already know that whatever it is I'm feeling will end the second Joy jets off in her rental car to the airport. It will have to. I'll catalogue it as a fever dream. Pretend I was sick on my holiday and had a bunch of demented visions.

"A penny for your thoughts," Joy's voice croaks next to me.

I turn to her, willing to move a bit more now that she's awake. I haven't slept in the same bed with another person since Alan left. "Morning." A smile breaks on my face at the sight of Joy's half-open sleep-crusted eyes. I guess I do have feelings for her.

"What time is it?" Joy asks, her eyes already falling shut again.

"Early. Go back to sleep." I trace a finger over her cheek, and the touch electrifies me.

"Okay," she says, "but, Alice, I was thinking that I should probably move my flight to Sunday."

"Yeah?" How can words so mundane touch me so deeply?

Joy just nods and crawls a bit closer towards me, pressing her cheek against my shoulder.

Now I surely can't move. So, I revel in her touch, and in the memories of last night. No wonder Joy is still sleepy. The sprinklers had already come on by the time we settled down and our bodies fell, exhausted, onto the mattress. I recall the look in her eyes when she came—so different from any of her other looks. Stripped of bravado with not the slightest bit of room for arrogance. Her head thrown back, her throat on display, her entire body a testament to how she was relinquishing to my touch. A display so addictive that, when I did finally crawl between her legs and lick her 'pussy' until she came, a sadness overcame me because I wasn't there with her when she climaxed, and the exquisite look on her face was lost to the world. When she made me climax later, a finger circling my clitoris insistently, at an ever-growing pace, her gaze locked on mine, it was hard for me to let go—although I did eventually. It was not an easy ask, and I contemplated begging her to look away, but instead I closed my eyes, and saw her face on the back of my eyelids anyway.

Then, as Joy's breathing slows, another question burrows to the forefront of my mind. Am I a lesbian? Was I completely honest when I told Joy I had never—never!—been attracted to another woman before? Could it be that I have the sort of personality that can suppress my most honest urges? While I know full well how uptight and focused on work and my daily routine I can be, I really don't think I would have denied myself that knowledge, at least not willingly.

I watch as the light slowly diffuses the darkness in my room, the darkness that protected me from the morning after. But this is not the cold hard light of day that's being shed upon us, upon this tableau of older woman in bed with younger woman after an unbelievable night together. It is warm Portuguese morning light, a dawn so soft and inviting, it makes me curl my toes in contentment, and slant my head until the side of it touches the top of Joy's unruly hair, and I wait patiently until she wakes up again.

"Hey," she says when she does. "Best morning I've had in quite some time." The light catches in her brown eyes, makes them glimmer.

"What do you want for breakfast?" I ask, because I truly don't know what else to say.

"You," she says, "but I may need a minute."

My cheeks flush. My skin burns. That's not what I meant, I want to say, because I'm not used to living in a world full of sexual innuendo, where my every word is turned into an invitation, but I remain silent, and look at the sunlight on Joy's face, and enjoy the unexpected rush of happiness that travels through me.

★ ★ ★

Later, when we do have breakfast, and the pool looks much bluer than the day before, and the sky seems even more spectacular than any time I've seen it in the days before Joy kissed me, and the breeze in the trees is just perfect, I ask her if she remembers what she said when she briefly woke up earlier.

"About changing my flight?" she asks. "Already taken care of. I called the airline while you were in the shower." At first, she had wanted to join me in the shower, but I desperately needed a few minutes by myself to cool off after waking up next to her. Needed to roam my hands over my body and re-assess it as mine. Stand in front of the mirror and check for signs of me. Alice McAllister. Solicitor. Fifty-one years old. Celibate for fifteen years. "Not anymore," I told my reflection.

"Really?" I watch Joy pop a piece of toast into her mouth and chew it triumphantly, if that is even a thing.

"I can't fuck you and leave you, Alice," she says with her mouth full, something that would have irritated me before. Now I find it endearing. Even when she uses the word *fuck*, which I most certainly haven't grown accustomed to yet, and doubt I ever will.

"What about your new job?" I find myself sounding like her mother when I ask that question.

"It doesn't start until Monday. I wanted to stay until Sunday in the first place, but Mum forbade me." Joy's mention of Miranda stiffens my limbs. How can I ever face her again? And how can I not when she will be the first person I see after I return, and the day after, and the day after. A person with question after question about my stay in her house, who will also grill me on how much of a nuisance her daughter was. A woman who probably, right at this moment, feels guilty for inflicting Joy's presence on me. A woman who knows me better than anyone in this world, and who will surely notice that something has changed, despite the fact I'll be extra careful not to reveal anything.

"Are you, uh, in touch with her at all? Does she text or call you?"

Joy sighs. "Don't worry about Mum, okay? I promise you, with my hand on my heart"—she puts her slice of toast down and puts her hand on her chest—"that Mum will never find out."

"You don't work with her every day." What started as a tingle of discomfort is quickly turning into a mountain of unsurmountable fear in my gut.

"Alice, Alice… listen to me. We have"—she stops to calculate—"three and a half days left. During that time, I'm going to make it my mission to relax you as much as possible. And right now, Mum is a faraway notion. She's not here. When she texts, I'll just tell her what I tell her every other day: that everything is fine. We're getting along well. So well, in fact, that you have given explicit permission for me to stay an extra two days. She's not a suspicious person. Never has been. For her, this is a good outcome. I had to beg her to come here. She'll be so chuffed to learn we've become friendly. No need to tell her exactly *how* friendly."

It's so easy to believe Joy when she declares things like that, as though her reasoning is the most logical and elegantly leads us to the only possible outcome.

"I understand your worry." Joy surprises me now. "But there's plenty of time for that later, like next week for instance, before you go back. It's a beautiful day." Her eyes scan the garden. "And I'm going to fuck you under that tree, Alice. As I live and breathe." Her gaze rests on the biggest tree at the far end of the garden. "I don't mean to be presumptuous, but I bet you haven't been initiated in the joys of al fresco loving." She faces me, her lips curved into a wide smile.

I shake my head at her, unable to suppress a grin. "I wish you wouldn't say things like that," I say, even if I don't mean it. But, it's as though if I cling to a modicum of decorum, I can at least pretend to control what is happening here. This seduction. This steamrollering over the person I have been my entire life. This metamorphosis.

"Things like what?" There's a smile in Joy's voice. "Al fresco?" She shrugs. "I always thought that was a perfectly acceptable word."

Joy is right, there's plenty of time to worry later, and I am glad that she's staying longer. Glad because of what it implies. She wants to be here with me longer. It's a flattering, blush-inducing thought. Stronger than the fear of returning, because this is now and going back is only for later.

"Hold on, Alice," Joy says, "I'm going to rock your world once more." She's so cocky, so overly confident it should put me off, but it does the opposite. It makes my legs turn to liquid, my muscles to jelly, my resistance into a faraway notion.

Joy has me pressed with my back against the tree she mentioned at breakfast. Its trunk is wide and rough, and scratches me when she leans in to kiss me again. I am not this person leaning against this tree, I think, this is not the Alice I know—the Alice I am. And it's true that in moments like these I don't recognise myself. I have become someone else. Someone who willingly goes along with silly ideas like being 'fucked' against a tree in my business partner's holiday house in the Algarve by her only daughter. It's easier when I think it's not me.

Joy's lips are by my ear now. I have noticed she never lets pass an opportunity to whisper something often crass but ultimately excruciatingly enticing in my ear. "You change when you come," she says now. "I can see your true self." This is not as much crass as it is upsetting. I do? But, of course I do. How can I not. When a climax thunders through me, I am not the Alice who wakes up at 6 a.m. every day. Who spends the first forty-five minutes of her day on the elliptical watching BBC breakfast, and arrives at the office every single weekday at 7.45 a.m. sharp—and more often than not on Saturdays as well.

And what is my true self? I wonder. Joy doesn't give me time to ponder this question. She sinks her teeth into my earlobe and even though it doesn't hurt as such, I flinch anyway. I can feel her lips stretch into a smile against the skin of my neck. I can feel how much she's enjoying this. This awakening of an old spinster she has set in motion. Because this is all Joy's doing. For the life of me, I would never have kissed her. I would probably never have even recognised the need within me to do so—even though the need, now, is great. So great, I pull her towards me and slip my tongue between her lips. Her naked breasts push against my flesh and my entire body has turned into one big pulsing mess once again.

Joy's lips leave mine and descend. She kneels in front of me and I only see the top of her hair, which is wild like her, and untamed, also like her. Joy is a wild child, unafraid to kiss her mother's friend again and again. Uninhibited by what's socially correct and all the rules I live by.

I spread my legs wide for her, pushing my back against the tree for support. It will leave scratches, I'm sure, but I honestly couldn't care less, because Joy's lips are already exploring my inner thigh, my outer lips, my clitoris… Her tongue dances around my most sensitive extremity again, and she does it so deftly, so confidently, she has my knees buckling in no time.

"I think it'll take about ten orgasms before you can truly, slowly enjoy the pleasures of love-making," she said earlier this afternoon after cornering me in the swimming pool, spreading my legs, and slipping her finger inside me.

"Ten?" I asked, my voice an astounded moan.

"I'm just fucking with you, Alice," she said afterwards. "Just making excuses to fuck you as many times as I can—not that I need an excuse for that."

Strangely, I've lost track. Is this the tenth I'm thundering towards? The fifth? The fifteenth? The cries of pleasure, the soft, warm clenching in my stomach just before, the sensation that even my skin has come alive under her touch, it has all blended into one long twenty-four hour climax in my brain.

Joy's tongue swirls around my clitoris, plunges into me, retreats and repeats. Her fingertips dig into my buttocks. But the sensation I'm most aware of is that I'm standing naked against a tree. It's a liberating feeling that has me giddy, has me twirling my fingers in her hair, has me pushing her against me more, because I can't get enough of this. The moment this stops, surely, I'll have to go back to the old me.

One last flick and my entire body goes rigid for an instant. I can feel Joy's breath on my sex before she pulls herself up, her face one big smile in front of mine.

"God, you're so easy, Alice," she says, and this gives me pause, because I certainly never used to be. I can't think of anyone I know on this earth who would describe me as easy in any context. But this is exactly what Joy has done, she has given me a new context to be myself in, a space to inhabit freely, a space for gentle teasing but never harsh judgement, a space where words like 'fucking' and 'pussy' and 'clit' are favoured over politeness and carefulness. Is that what she meant when she said she can see my true self? I wonder what that woman looks like. I guess, for starters, she's naked against a tree.

This afternoon, when we were both lounging by the pool, exhausted but sated, when I let my mind drift while I closed my eyes, images I have never seen before projected themselves on the big screen in my mind. Slices of imagery I never knew existed. Images of Joy's behind offered to me, and me doing unimaginable things to it. I have no idea where these images came from, although I can only conclude they ascended from the deepest recesses of my subconscious mind.

Almost, I ask her to position herself on all fours on the grass in front of me. Just because she's so cocky and self-assured, and she's as good as begging for it. But I can't. I don't have it in me. I'm not Joy. I don't ask for things like that. I wait until they come to me.

"I am easy with you," I reply.

"Like putty in my hands," she says.

"Perhaps." I pull her closer and, as I do, another image makes its way forwards. A moving image of me and Joy at Sagres, blue sky all around us, and she's holding my hand.

CHAPTER ELEVEN

It's Sunday morning and my stomach is bunched together with dread. Joy is packing up her few belongings in her room. Her plane leaves at midday. She has to leave in one hour. She told me it would be foolish to follow her to the airport in my rental car, that it would be far better to say our goodbyes here, in private.

I sit on my bed—the bed where everything changed—and let my gaze drift over the pool the way it did when she first jumped into it topless. The past few days, all we've done is sunbathe topless. I try to remember how it vexed me, how it cramped me up, how unseemly I thought it the first time.

A knock on the open door startles me. "Hey," Joy says. "We should probably talk."

We should, because we have done anything but talk in the past four days. We drank sangria, gin and tonic, and wine. We grilled squid and sardines on the barbecue. We basked in post-orgasmic glory. We fucked against the tree two more times, and in the pool after dusk, and in the sea only last night. We slept with our skin glued to each other, our limbs entangled, and my mind fuller and fuller with images of a future that's impossible. But now that I have experienced the other me, and as the days have progressed, I find it hard to go back to my former self. I'm meant to stay here for five more days, all on my own, with only Joy's memory to keep me company. It's bewildering how, after a lifetime of being untouched, a mere few days can leave me so in need of more. Of her lips against my shoulder when she kisses me good morning. Of her finger circling my belly button before it meanders down. Of her hand gently squeezing my shoulder when she offers me a glass of wine.

"Are you all set?"

Joy nods and heads towards me, sits down next to me on the bed. "I know this is hard." She leans her head on my shoulder.

"It is what it is." A phrase so devoid of meaning, it seems like an utter waste of time in the hour we have left together.

"It was glorious and refreshing and restorative and bloody satisfying," Joy says, "and now it's hard."

"It was a holiday… thing." I can hardly use the word 'love'.

"Look, Alice, I've been thinking," Joy starts, then turns towards me. "Holiday thing or not, we live in the same city. I mean, we could see each other if we wanted to." Never has Joy's voice sounded so robbed of confidence. She might be a tad arrogant and very self-assured, but she's not stupid.

"I think we both know that's not an option. We can't even tell anyone about this. No one, okay?"

"It's our dirty little secret." Joy reaches for my hand and takes it in hers. "I'm going to miss you."

God, me too, I want to say, but this is no time to be overly dramatic. "You have so many things to look forward to, Joy. A new job. New people in your life. A new routine." And as I sum up all the new things Joy has to look forward to, in my head, I recite all the actions that make up my old routine—all the things I don't have to look forward to. All I see when I think of my elliptical, of many a dinner consumed on my own, of arriving at the office before anyone else, is a loneliness I don't know how to handle.

"But you, Alice." Joy's voice is still soft, careful. "You only have one life and it's now."

Inwardly, I chuckle at the generic phrase she utters. I chuckle because otherwise I might cry, because what she says is true.

"What are you going to do when you get back?" Joy asks.

"Get on with my life." Even as I say the words, they sound so hollow and untrue. "Go back to work. Do what I always do."

"Promise me you'll do more fun things. More out-of-the-box activities."

This time I chuckle audibly. "Such as?" While we're having this meandering, ultimately going-nowhere conversation, dread multiplies in my gut. The fact of the matter is that I don't want Joy to go. I'm afraid of how I'll feel once her car drives off the driveway. Whatever will I do with myself? Perhaps I should check in with work. It feels like months since I last really thought about one of my clients, like something I did in a different life.

"Go to a Bruce Springsteen concert," she says. "And look out for me." She looks at me from under her lashes. "Look, Alice, I know you have many perfectly plausible reasons why this can't work. I understand that. I won't ask you to sum them up so I can contest them. It's hardly the time for that now. But, I want you to know that it's different for me. I don't care who frowns upon who I'm with. I truly, honestly don't give a toss. Because it's my life, and no one else's, and when I see a chance at happiness, I grab it. That's the kind of person I am. I know you're different, and I respect that, but all I'm asking is that you leave the door open just a fraction." She holds up her hand, her thumb and index finger an inch apart. "This much."

And now I can't hold the question in any longer. It was easy enough at first and under the circumstances, but now that she's expressly alluding to life after this holiday fling, I need to know. "I'm flattered that you would even ask, Joy, but really, what's in it for you? I'm in my fifties. What do I have to offer a girl like you, with the world at her feet?"

She scrunches her lips into a pensive pout before speaking. "I normally wouldn't answer that question because it's so bloody obvious, but for you I will." She puts a hand on my knee. "I assume not many people are aware of this. Hell, I even assume you're not aware of it, but beneath that stubborn coating of properness, and righteousness, and work ethic, and being a lady and all that, you are a stunning, kind, passionate and sexy woman, Alice. I've seen it. At first I was just teasing you, trying to draw you out, but I saw something brewing within you. Behind those ever careful eyes of yours, behind your ever polite behaviour. I mean, yes, I have a thing for older women, but, for the life of me, I never expected this to happen. I never thought I would be sitting here with you, saying goodbye, and it being so bloody hard, because I don't want to say goodbye."

"Neither do I," I blurt out, overtaken by emotion and so immensely touched by Joy's words, by her sweet assessment of me, that, if it were an option at all, I'd pack my own bags, go to the airport, and hop on the plane to London with her.

"Your turn, Alice." Joy changes the tone of the moment by using a cheerful voice. "What does a successful, patient—and I know this because you've been best friends with my mum forever so you must have inexhaustible amounts of it—and accomplished woman like yourself want with the likes of me? With someone who had to quit her job because she slept with her boss? With someone with no discernible career path and no immediate desire to even pursue a career?"

We haven't discussed work much. We haven't discussed many things much. Yet, the answer to Joy's question is staggeringly easy. "You're absolutely gorgeous and so… so alive. So funny and such a force, such a bundle of energy. You thoroughly rocked my world when you arrived." If anything, this is Miranda's fault, I think out of the blue, my brain frantically looking for excuses. It's her fault for allowing Joy to come here.

Joy turns fully towards me, her big brown eyes scanning

my face, her expressive eyebrows perked up. "Promise me one thing. Just one little thing. Promise me you'll at least think about it. For all we know, this really is just something that happened while we were on holiday, something that could only occur under a Southern-European blue sky, where inhibitions are so easily cast aside, and it won't stand a chance in real life. It could be. But I think we owe it to what has happened here to at least ask ourselves: what if? What if it's more than that, Alice? What if it's more and we just walk away?"

I have no recourse. Joy has certainly inherited Miranda's argument skills. Miranda always wanted her to become a lawyer like herself. She would have made an excellent one.

"I promise," is all I say.

"Thank you." Joy scuttles closer, nearly onto my lap, and starts pushing me down onto the bed. "Now enough of this depressing stuff. We have fifteen minutes left for kissing and other things." Her lips find mine in a flash, and all the time her mouth is on mine, her tongue inside, I can only think about how this is our very last kiss, and how much I don't want it to be.

I stand at the gates of Miranda's property for a long time after Joy's car has vanished. She's gone. She's actually gone. Whatever will I do now? Finally learn how to successfully masturbate? Only yesterday Joy asked me to touch myself while she watched and, while I was willing to go very far for her, and she broke through many of my boundaries, I had to draw the line somewhere. But, as I keep standing there for a while longer, as though willing her yellow Mini to return to me and undo this knot in my stomach, I know this isn't all about my sexual reawakening. It's about these feelings she has stirred in me, and how I have absolutely no means to deal with them.

CHAPTER TWELVE

On Friday I'm at the airport hours before my plane is set to leave, but I couldn't stay at the house any longer. Although Miranda assured me a cleaner would come by after I had vacated, the place is spic-and-span. Not a shred of evidence is left of my stay there—and what happened during it.

Unlike when I picked up the car from the rental agency, returning it is a breeze. Faro airport is poorly air-conditioned, small, and, because it's a holiday destination, full of couples and families.

The question that's been nagging me the most since Joy left is why I chose to be alone. Because, at some point in my life, it must have been more than just a subconscious choice, something that happened, more than a logical consequence of the sort of life I lived and the aspirations I had. Why, after Alan, did I not let anyone else in? I've come up with many possible answers—the divorce must have traumatised me more than I knew; I didn't have time; I had no interest in the men who pursued me; I was secretly a repressed lesbian; I valued my privacy and my routine too much—but none of them conclusive.

I find a seat in a noisy replica of an Irish pub and order a glass of wine. Joy's words have echoed in my head constantly, but no matter how nicely she put it, how eloquently she delivered the message, and how much, in an ideal world, I would want to 'leave the door ajar', it's simply not an option. I have examined the issue from every possible angle. I sat at the patio table, overlooking the pool now devoid of life, with a sheet of blank paper in front of me and a blue and red pen, listing pros and cons. There was only one pro; there were many cons.

Happiness. That was the pro. The only word written in blue, flanked by a long list of what it would cost me. Miranda. The company. A life-long friendship and the accompanying trust. My life as I know it and that I lived, if not with zest, at the very least always with dignity and respect for others and myself. At the bottom of the sheet of paper, I'd written in big red letters: it's simply not possible. Then I burned it to remove all trace of it.

I hear my phone beep in my purse. I know it's Joy. She has texted me every day since she left. Nothing untoward—nothing that, if Miranda were to accidentally find her phone and read the messages, would cause suspicion. Just short messages to check in with me, as she put it in her first text. I have never replied. Because replying would be the first step to giving in, to believing in Joy's fantasy. And she may not care what others think of her, but I certainly do. My reputation is all I have. And gosh, the number of middle-aged male lawyers I have known to sleep with their twenty-years-younger paralegals and assistants over the course of my career. There is no way I would ever want to be lumped in with the likes of them, because I have always found them profoundly pathetic—perhaps even more so because Alan left me for a younger woman as well.

I dig my mobile from my bag and read Joy's message: *Have a safe flight back. J. xo*

A harmless enough note. She's persistent, though. Tenacious, like Miranda—and like me. Last night, I drank almost an entire bottle of wine by myself and tried to imagine breaking the news to Miranda. I imagined her face. The look of disgust and disbelief. The judgement. I put myself in her place and cursed myself for being so weak, because, no matter how much I hide what happened with Joy, it *did* happen. I have slept with Miranda's daughter—and thoroughly enjoyed it at that. I deserve only punishment for that. I certainly don't deserve to be rewarded with happiness. The truth is that, despite my promise to Joy to keep an open mind, to allow a sliver of hope to permeate my thoughts about the future, I put a lid on that the very day she left. I had to. But it stings, because to have to actively conceal—to have to pretend it never even happened—one of the very best experiences of my life, is a painful matter.

As always, I don't reply to her message. I don't delete it yet—I will do that on Sunday, before returning to work on Monday. Before I face Miranda. She tried to call me last Thursday, but I couldn't pick up. I just texted her an hour later saying I was out and missed her call and everything was fine. But when her number appeared on my phone screen, the first thought in my head was that Joy let something slip and Miranda was calling to give me a piece of her mind. I realise this will be my first instinct for a while. I want to trust Joy to not spill the beans, but she's young and reckless and she drinks too much. And what if she gets in a fight with Miranda one day and, as an act of revenge, just blurts it out? I have no choice but to put my faith in her. The other option —coming clean—is not even a possibility.

So, I wait for my plane and drink two more glasses of wine. Excessive drinking is a habit I will get rid of as soon as I arrive home, but for now, I'm still abiding somewhat by Joy's words. You only live once.

As soon as the plane takes off, I fall asleep and I dream that Miranda finally tells me that Joy is a lesbian and has a girlfriend. Miranda looks happy so I know that the girlfriend she's referring to is certainly not me. But it's a dream, so Miranda nudges me in the arm and says, "you old dog, you." Then I wake up.

✳ ✳ ✳

On Monday before work, instead of my usual forty-five minutes on the elliptical, I work out for an hour. I still arrive half an hour before my usual time, and the office is quiet and peaceful. To my big surprise, Miranda walks in five minutes before eight.

"Alice, hello!" She spreads her arms wide for a hug and already I feel like I'm dying a little inside, like I betrayed my best friend in the very worst way, and I wasn't able to feel the full extent of the grief I caused until I looked her in the eyes. She tried to call me again over the weekend, but I just stared at my phone in horror, thinking: *this is it*. "You're a difficult woman to get hold of these days, but I can only assume that's a good thing." I used to be in the habit of picking up my phone after the first ring. "I hope you had a wonderful time."

"I did. Thank you so much for letting me stay in your house. It's gorgeous."

"It's such a relief. I was very worried about Joy turning up like that. I'm so glad you got along. Mind you, my daughter is quite an easy person to be around, but she does have her ways." Miranda squeezes my shoulder. "But she told me you and she had a jolly time together."

"We did. It was no nuisance at all," I reply, and I find it easier to lie than I had expected, although what I'm saying isn't a lie as such. "She's a lovely girl."

"Well, seeing as you enjoyed each other's company so much, Joy suggested I'd invite you both to dinner on Friday."

Instinctively, I flinch, retreating like someone is trying to slap me in the face. What is Joy playing at? I have no time to consider this, though, because I need to refuse Miranda's invitation as quickly and efficiently as possible. "Thank you very much for inviting me, but that's really not necessary. Besides, I have so much work to catch up on, I don't think I'll be able to make it."

Miranda widens her stance and crosses her arms in front of her chest. "It's funny, but Joy predicted you would say that. As did I, by the way. The point of a holiday is not to undo all its effects the instant you come back, you know? There's absolutely no way you are working after eight o'clock on Friday. My daughter also firmly instructed me to not let you get away with lame excuses like that. She must have got to know you pretty well, huh?" Miranda extends an arm and pats me patronisingly on the upper arm.

What is this? An emotional sting operation organised by Joy to make me have a nervous breakdown? And what am I supposed to say now? Will it be more suspicious if I try to get out of it more, or should I just accept? "I'll check my calendar, Miranda, but I can't make any promises." I try to buy myself some time.

"It's just dinner, Alice. You used to come to dinner at my house all the time, remember?"

"I do, although not as fondly as I would if you hadn't tried to set me up with Lionel Ashley a dozen times."

"You aren't still cross about that, are you? That was years ago. I think it's time to reinstate the tradition. And I swear it'll just be the four of us. No set-ups."

"I'll let you know." It's not in my nature to budge now.

"I'll take that as a yes, either way." Miranda smiles and I see so much of Joy in her smile it's more like a blow to the stomach. "Nice tan, by the way, Alice. You look good. You have that post-holiday glow about you. I like it."

"Thank you," I mumble, figuring that not a lot of that glow will be left after a few more of these conversations.

"Let's do lunch, okay? We have a lot to catch up on." Miranda walks to her office and I realise that, just like Joy, she is so used to always getting her own way. She has no idea that in this case accomplishing that may leave her very upset.

✶ ✶ ✶

The familiarity of work is soothing to my nerves, and I even make it through most of lunch with Miranda without breaking out in cold sweats. We mainly talk about clients and matters she has handled in my absence, until the topic of conversation turns to Joy. Miranda talks about how the first week at her new job was promising, that Joy has told her the people were nice and the work challenging but interesting— for now, she adds, with an eye-roll—and I just have to ask.

"Speaking of Joy," I say, and my voice trembles a little when I say her name. I'll need to work on that. "Why did you never tell me that she is a, uh, lesbian?" Why is it so hard for me to say that word?

Miranda sighs. "Two reasons, I guess. First, I know you well enough to know you don't like discussing very personal things like that. It makes you blush and stammer and you always tend to change the topic quickly." Miranda clearly doesn't mean this as an insult as she just continues. And while it's true that I do like to keep a polite distance, and I value discretion, I can't help but take offence a little. "Second, it's not as if she's ever been with anyone serious. Meaning longer than a few months. And, yes, I confess, it took me some time to adjust to the notion, but I have now. I just want her to be happy. I'm fifty-eight years old, Alice, and truly, that girl's happiness is all I want from my life at this point. She doesn't make it easy on herself, though. Let's just say she has a bit of a flawed taste in women."

I'm suddenly grateful Miranda lost the habit of discussing personal matters with me because this *is* making me highly uncomfortable. The remark about flawed taste doesn't help. "Oh really?" I ask, though, because this is Joy we're talking about and, despite myself, despite the resolve I have spent the entire weekend building up, I want to know more.

"She had an affair with her boss at her last job. It's why she quit." Miranda takes a gulp of wine. "While the pair of you were in Quinta, did Joy say anything about me, er, being a bad sport about accepting her being gay? I don't mean to be, I really don't, but Joy isn't exactly the most patient person in the world and, well, I'm doing the best I can. Next time she's seeing someone I will reserve judgement until I've met the person. I will be open-minded and non-judgemental, and will only focus on how happy this woman is making my daughter. I just wish she was more interested in girls her own age, you know? It's hard enough as it is, but of course Joy needs to go after older women, as well. She likes to make things hard on herself, just like her father used to." Miranda gives a nervous smile after her monologue. "Sorry, I'm rambling. I know better than to ask you to be indiscreet, Alice. Please ignore my question. That was just the worried mother in me rearing her head."

"She said nothing of the sort," I hear myself saying. I don't know why I lie. Perhaps to calm Miranda down, or to make her feel better about herself, or to give the indication that Joy and I didn't discuss personal matters. Either way, it's a dishonest deflection, and it makes me feel like a terrible person. Half a day back on the job has made me lie to my best friend already.

"Thank you for saying that," Miranda says and she sounds genuinely grateful, like I've just done her the biggest favour in the world. If only she knew.

CHAPTER THIRTEEN

When I ring Miranda's doorbell on Friday evening at eight o'clock sharp, it's Joy who opens the door—of course it is. Throughout the week, I had to suppress the urge to text her many times per day to ask her what she was playing at, but I felt safer pretending I didn't know what it was all about. In the end, I figured a confrontation with Joy was bound to happen at some point, and this way it can be over and done with quickly, and I can get on with my life. Despite the agony of carrying around a secret like this, work has normalised my emotions. I have found relief in my routine and, although I do lie awake at night more often than before, with images of Joy launching endless assaults on the back of my closed eyelids, it's a manageable nuisance now that I'm back in my comfort zone.

"Hey," she says, the way she always did in Quinta, and I feel my resolve melt into a puddle. She leans one shoulder against the door frame. It's funny at first to see her with so many clothes on. In jeans and a blouse she almost looks like a different person. But, of course, she's not. She's still Joy with that beaming smile, and those bottomless eyes, and that tone of voice that undoes me a bit. I quickly realise I've made a big mistake coming here. "Come in." She steps aside.

I can still turn around, I think. This situation can be avoided. But it's as though I'm under Joy's spell again—another way I have started to look at the goings-on in Quinta—and I suddenly need to spend a little time in her company. So, I straighten my spine and tell myself this will be the vaccine I need. Ingest a small portion of the poison that will make me battle-ready to fight it later on.

"I've missed you," she whispers as I pass her in the hallway.

I want to say something in return, but I'm in Miranda's house and Jeff's booming laughter coming from the other room holds me back. I just give her a stare which I hope is menacing, but I realise is probably as wanton as when she fucked me against that tree.

I head farther into the house, taking deep breaths, reminding myself to act normal. Joy and I are supposed to be friendly with each other. That's one of the reasons I'm here.

"I figured you would have something better to do on a Friday night than have dinner with the likes of us," I say to Joy after having kissed Miranda and Jeff hello.

"Nonsense. Besides, I owe you the pleasure of my company to make up for crashing your holiday." She smiles a smile I can't read, more of a smirk, really. What does she mean, anyway? Perhaps I should have contacted her beforehand. Or feigned sudden illness after leaving work. My stomach is upset enough. "I'll take that." She reaches for the bottle of wine that I'm still carrying and puts a hand on mine. Our eyes meet and I have a choice between crumbling, dissolving at her touch, or steeling myself the way I do when I'm about to persuade a potential client to hire us. If Joy has invited me here to play a game, she's in for a treat. I haven't become the lawyer I am today by giving in easily.

"Thank you," I say and, not smiling, give her the bottle.

"Jeff is on cooking duty tonight." Miranda heads into the living room with a tray of pistachios and a ripe and oozing Brie. "So we can just relax and gossip." Miranda winks at me because she knows how much I hate talking behind other people's backs. "Please, sit."

I know this house so well, and have spent so much time here over the years, but I find myself looking around for a seat, as if I've lost my bearings.

"G&T?" Joy asks. "I'm on drinks duty so Mum can just relax and be a princess." She curls an arm around her mother's shoulder and squeezes it before heading to the kitchen without waiting for my reply.

Her head peeks out from around the kitchen door. "Yes?" She eyes me again, her stare bold and piercing.

"Sure," I say, because I could sure do with something to take the edge off right now.

Miranda and I talk about work briefly, until Joy re-enters the living room with three tall glasses. "Enough shop talk, I command you," she says, as she deposits the drinks on the coffee table. "It's the weekend, for heaven's sake. There's more to life than work. Did you know, for instance, Mum, that Alice has much better taste in music than you?"

Already, I feel a drop of sweat making its way down my spine. But Miranda has no reason to not take the quip in jest. "Yes, Alice is superior to me in many ways, I'm well aware." Miranda picks up her glass and holds it out so I can tap mine against it.

Joy sits down next to Miranda and doesn't take her eyes off me.

"Am I allowed to inquire about your new job?" I ask her, my voice sounding too insecure for my liking.

"Oh, it's fine. It's basically the same as what I did before, except for other companies and with different co-workers. It's not rocket science, but it pays the bills."

"It's never too late to get your law degree, darling. Stephen's son did just that and he's working for us now." Miranda is not in a position to see how Joy rolls her eyes.

"You'd go mad if I worked for you," Joy says to Miranda. "I'd challenge you at every turn and wouldn't take any shit."

"Language, dear," Miranda is quick to say, but I can tell she's just toying with Joy, the way Joy is with her. It's clear how much Miranda enjoys her daughter's company. How easy they are around each other.

"Oops, better wash my mouth," Joy says and takes a large gulp of her drink.

We talk back and forth like that for a while. Nothing harmful is being said and Joy behaves, until Jeff invites us to the table. I'm seated opposite Joy and, as soon as I sit down, I feel a toe against my ankle, then slowly crawling up my shin. Stupidly, I look around, but it can, of course, only be Joy, because Jeff and Miranda are busy serving food and replenishing drinks. When I work up the nerve to look at Joy, her chin is resting on her fist and her eyes shimmer with something that is about to drive me mad. But it's not her gaze undoing me, it's the touch of her foot against my leg—burning through my stockings. It doesn't matter. I might as well be wearing a knight's armour, I'd still feel the heat of it shooting up my flesh. And then I know that Joy has used her own mother to seduce me. Perhaps it's payback for not replying to her texts, or for not getting in touch—even though I never made such a promise—because of the vague pact we made to keep an open mind. Perhaps from my lack of response she deduced that involving her mother was the only way to see me, and to make clear that she still wants me. But, despite what seeing her, and feeling her toe now close to my knee, does to me, I find her tactics wholly disrespectful. What if Miranda does find out some day and realises what was happening underneath her dinner table? The very table she's about to feed us on.

It's also disrespectful towards me and my desires. Surely Joy knows that if I had wanted to see her, I would have been in touch. Or perhaps that's the problem. Although I have been pining for her since she left Portugal, I haven't made that clear at all. Or perhaps it's simply lack of attention.

For now, I have no choice but to tap into my steely reserve again and get through dinner. I don't have to stay late. I'm exhausted enough after a week back at work and insufficient sleep. I hope Jeff hasn't made dessert. Since when did he become such a chef, anyway?

Once we start eating, Joy's foot retreats, and Jeff talks about his job as a hedge fund manager the way he always does—like it's the single most important activity on earth—but, nevertheless, I focus my attention on him, and ask him questions indicating I'm interested in what he has to say, to avoid the conversation flowing into a direction I can't handle.

In between the first course and the main, I excuse myself to wash my hands—and splash some cold water in my face. I look at my reflection in the bathroom mirror for long seconds, telling myself to get a grip, even though outwardly, I think I'm giving a good enough performance to convince Miranda that I'm not coming apart at the seams because of Joy's trickery. An oblivious mind is easily fooled.

Once I've perked myself up enough to face Joy again, I open the bathroom door only to find her waiting for me in the hallway. Before I can say anything, she brings a finger to my lips, quieting me.

"Don't speak," she whispers. "Just nod yes or no."

The touch of her finger against my lips has me so flummoxed I'm nodding already.

"Please, meet me somewhere after dinner. I need to speak with you. Please." Her facial expression is sincere, and she stands so close to me, her body heat radiating onto my flesh, her perfume drifting up into my nose, I couldn't say no if I wanted to.

"Fine," I whisper, against her instructions to simply nod, "but only if you stop touching me under the table."

She cocks her head and gives a small smile. "Deal," she says.

★ ★ ★

After I've said my goodbyes and thanked Jeff and Miranda for dinner, kissing both of them *and* Joy briefly on the cheek, I walk slowly to the end of Miranda's street. My own house is only a ten-minute walk away. I don't look back. And in those few minutes I don't know if I want Joy to actually come after me, because that's what I suspect she will do. Say her own goodbye to Miranda and Jeff and come find me. If she does find me before I get home, and starts talking to me, starts getting under my skin, I'm not sure what will happen next. One of my specialties is hiding my thoughts behind an impassive mask—it's practically a job requirement. But just because I kept a straight face and conversed fluently with my hosts, doesn't mean that I wasn't falling apart on the inside.

Soon enough I hear a pair of footsteps approaching, and it makes me think about Joy's foot on my leg, her toes running along my calf. When I got up from the table, I was afraid her shenanigans would have left a run in my stocking. I slow my step, let her catch up with me.

"Hey," she says again. And when she says it now, it's as though I'm only just now absorbing the shock of seeing her again, of standing face-to-face with the woman who unpeeled layer after layer of my indestructible guard in Portugal.

"Let's go to my house," I whisper, ridiculously afraid of being overheard. "Where no one can see us."

"Sure." Side by side, wrapped in a tension-laden silence, we make our way to my house and as soon as we walk in, I feel as though I can properly exhale for the first time tonight.

"What you did was so unfair," I start to say to Joy. "You basically entrapped me."

"You could have tried harder to decline the invitation, Alice," Joy says as if me showing up at Miranda's house regardless is the biggest giveaway about my feelings.

"God, you're so arrogant. So incredibly cocky. Do you have any idea how being in that situation made me feel?"

"I'm sorry, Alice. I wanted to see you. And I wanted to make you see that being in the same room with Mum and me together would not instigate the end of the world."

I can only shake my head, because, as far as I can tell, she has only reached the exact opposite result. "What were you thinking?" I ask, after a few mute seconds have passed.

"The fuck if I know, Alice... All I know is that I can't stop thinking about you. And every day, I try to convince myself it's wrong, and every day, I'm more convinced that it's not." Joy is the one crumbling now and I see something new in her eyes. Agony. A need unmet. And I wish I could do something about it, and I also realise that my age is an advantage here. I've had to suck up so many things over the course of my life. And it's never easy when you can't have something you desperately want, and it always comes at a price, and there's no way I can impart this knowledge to Joy in the state she's in now.

"Let's sit for a bit," I say, and I have to keep myself from touching her, from just putting my hand on her shoulder in a friendly manner. I know it's better not to. Not just because it could be misinterpreted, but also because I don't trust myself around her. By the end of Joy's stay in Portugal, the briefest of touches could so easily lead to so much more.

We head into the lounge. "Do you want some water?" I ask.

"No, but a glass of wine would be nice."

When I stare at her too long, Joy asks, "What?"

I shake my head and fetch an open bottle I started the day before from the kitchen, pour us both a small glass and sit on the couch.

"I'm sorry I ignored your messages. I wasn't taking your feelings into account when I did. Only my own. That wasn't fair," I start, unsure of my moves on this unknown, treacherous terrain.

"And *I* am sorry for making you come to dinner. It was out of my mouth before I even realised, and I certainly didn't think it through. I was just focused on seeing you again, and then Mum ran with the idea, because why wouldn't she?"

"You haven't told her anything?" I'm glad to have a

glass of wine in my hands. It gives me something to do with them and I need all the courage I can get, liquid or other.

"Of course not. I swear to you, Alice. She doesn't have a clue."

"I can barely look her in the eye," I mumble. "I feel like the worst person to have ever walked this earth."

"Why?" Joy challenges me. "You haven't murdered anyone. You haven't committed a crime. We're not cheating on anyone. We are two consenting adults. I know you and Mum are close, but it's not as if we're related. We fell in love, Alice, it's as simple as that. And there's absolutely nothing wrong with that."

Her use of the word love jars me. Am I in love? I haven't a clue. I haven't been in love in decades. My heart feels as if it's in tatters. And I don't get much sleep. And too many thoughts are spent chasing off images of Joy.

When I don't reply, Joy puts down her glass of wine and walks over to crouch next to me. "Is asking for one date too much? Just one evening spent in each other's company, just to see how it makes us feel. To see if, under other circumstances, we would want to be together. One night during which we pretend I'm not your best friend's daughter."

"No, Joy. I can't. I want to, but I just can't. It's hard enough seeing you tonight. It brought back every single moment we spent together, and it will only make things harder in the end. I know it's not what you want to hear, and I wish I didn't have to speak these words, that I didn't have to refuse because, by God, it's hard. But it's not right."

"One date is all I ask. A mere two to three hours of your life. That's it. If you still feel the same way after that, I'll walk away. I swear to God, Alice, I will walk away from you, but please. We had such an amazing time. It was so special, and, for the life of me, I can't figure out why, but there's something between us and I know you feel it, too. You can't deny that. I just know it." She kneels next to me, as if she's going to beg, but instead she moves her hand from the armrest of the sofa to my thigh, and digs her fingertips into my flesh. I might as well just have been administered electric shock therapy, that's how her touch jolts through me, all the way from my thigh, up my spine, and back down again, between my legs.

I find myself gasping for air as I open my mouth to speak. "I—I'm not denying anything," I stutter and she must know she has me now, must know that I'm about to be putty in her hands again.

"Tomorrow night?" her fingers crawl to the pit of my knee, just below where my skirt has hiked up, and she strokes me there, and I feel myself go wet like a river.

"God, you really can't take no for an answer." I find her hand with mine, stop it in its tracks. She's got me so far that I'm ready to ask her to stay. And I realise that, yes, I must be falling in love, because why else would I be behaving like a clueless teenager whose behaviour is solely ruled by hormones?

"Some things are worth fighting for." Joy's fingers intertwine with mine, and she brings both our hands to her mouth, and kisses me on the tip of my index finger.

"What do you want to do on this date?" Back in the day, when Alan was courting me, it wasn't called dating yet.

"Go to a movie, or a play, and have dinner. We can go ice skating, or to the opera, or the library for all I care, Alice. I just want to spend time with you."

"We don't have to decide now, I guess." I hope not because I'm about to lose use of my faculties if she keeps her mouth hovering over my finger like that.

"If I call you tomorrow, will you pick up?" She eyes me from below.

"I will."

"Good." She thrusts herself up and stands over me, before lowering her head towards me and kissing me full on the lips. Instantly, my mouth opens, and I want more. I am at the same time angry at myself for being so weak, but, in this moment, I also very much want to believe Joy's argument. No one gets hurt when we kiss. No earthquakes destroy the world when my tongue slips into her mouth. Just as the kiss is about to intensify, Joy pulls back. "I'll see you tomorrow then." She pushes herself away from me and just stands there with a crooked grin on her lips. "I'll see myself out."

Just as on our last day together in Quinta, I watch the spot where she stood for a long time before I can move again.

CHAPTER FOURTEEN

It's almost indecent how, from the very beginning of our date, all I want to do is take Joy home. When she called me earlier today, and I picked up after the first ring, I invited her to my house. Not only because of what I want to do to her —and have her do to me—but also because I was paranoid about actually going out with her, to a place where we could be seen.

"There are eight million people living in this city, Alice," she said. "And we're not staying in Chelsea, I can assure you."

At seven, I meet Joy at a wine bar in Shoreditch, a neighbourhood so unfamiliar to me, I might as well be in another city.

"My flat is just around the corner," she says, and this piques my interest because I'm curious to find out how Joy lives. I'm also pleased that, if we do want more privacy, we don't have to go all the way back to Chelsea. "Welcome to my hood, Alice." I am, naturally, also worried, because if this is Joy's *hood*, as she calls it, she must know people here. "Don't worry, none of my friends would ever set foot in this overpriced, snobbish place. We're safe."

"What would you say if one of them did, though? If one of them is sneaking around with someone as well, and had decided to bring them here. How would you introduce me?" I feel giddy sitting across from her. Radiating. Eager.

"I would say 'I'm very pleased to present to you... my brand new cougar'." Joy snickers, obviously finding herself very funny. "I'm not ashamed to be seen with you, just for the record. I just wanted to bring you to the most discreet bar. Afterwards, we can either pick up a curry and eat it at mine, or go to a very nice restaurant across from the park. We'll see how things go."

"Right." How things go? Once again, I'm thrown by the effect she has on me. By how she has me second-guessing my every word, my every gesture, my every emotion. Perhaps she was right and this is what being in love feels like. I've found that additional symptoms include waking up an hour before my alarm goes off despite interrupted sleep due to a new set of worries. My mind also tends to drift when it should be fully engaged listening to clients or even the morning news—I find myself unable to recall a single one of today's headlines. And then there's the spring in my step I only noticed on my way over here, not when I was running errands this afternoon.

"What do you think of the wine, Alice?" Joy asks. It comes across not so much as a question but an invitation to gaze into her eyes, to relish this moment we have together and act as though it's normal, all while absorbing the energy of her smile and the relentless sparkle in her gaze. If someone asked me to paint a picture of an infatuated woman, I'd paint what I'm looking at right now. It's a delight to notice the twitch in the corner of her mouth, and the way she—ever so slightly—drags the tip of her tongue over her bottom lip. Joy is in full-on seduction mode, so full-on and obliterating that, after only fifteen minutes of sitting in this bar with her, I find myself not caring about any consequences. And I know it's also because of the wine she keeps pouring generously from the bottle she ordered, but it's by no means the main cause. This girl—woman, really— has done something to me. She has turned me inside out and unearthed desires in me I was so unaware of, that I was willing to spend the rest of my life, to go into my old age, fully ignoring them.

"What have you done to me?" I had asked Joy for the

umpteenth time when I lay gasping on top of the covers in the house in Quinta. "I'm not like this. I'm not this person lying here."

"The woman who just came so violently it seemed like the devil itself was being exorcised from her soul?" Joy lay on her belly looking at me, that ever-present grin on her face.

"I don't recognise myself. You must have poisoned me, put something in that wine you poured me the first day. A slow-working potion that is messing with my judgement and my brain chemistry and… basically with every cell of my being,."

"What can I say, Alice? You saw a pair of bare breasts and you flipped. It's hardly my fault."

"It's not that," I said, my voice growing more serious, "it was just the sight of you and what it stood for in my mind. You're so unbridled, so uninhibited, so completely the opposite of me, I couldn't believe it at first. I found myself wondering: really? This is how youngsters are these days? They walk into a house, greet someone whom they haven't seen in years, and take their top off? It stood for something I couldn't grasp, something I couldn't possibly wrap my head around, until I did and you struck me as so beautiful, so pure and unspoiled, so devoid of delusion and signs of what simply living your life can do to you."

"Well, Alice." Joy still had that grin on her face. "I hate to break it to you but I'm neither pure, nor unspoiled, and, well, I think you were just horny." She broke out in a giggle and hoisted herself up on her arms to kiss me on the nose and on the lips again.

"God, you're so disrespectful," I said to her when we broke from the kiss.

"And you love it," she replied, and started making her way down between my legs again.

"I think the wine is delicious," I say now, while I lose the first layer of my defence. "And I also think we should skip dinner altogether."

"Do you now?" Joy huddles over the table conspiratorially. "Don't you have to give me a lecture first to make yourself feel better?" There's no malice in her voice. She's teasing me, testing me.

I drink my wine, my eyes still on her, and I think to myself: what if this *is* me? What if this is the Alice I've always been and I've wasted years hiding her? I need to get out of this bar now and find out.

"I think you must have put the same potion in my drink again. The one that makes me cross all my boundaries, far and beyond." My eyes stray to her neck, to the hollow of it, and how the boat neck top she's wearing makes it stand out so that I want to press my lips to it and kiss it endlessly.

"Well, if my potion is working then I guess I'd better take you home." Joy puts her hand on the table, looks at it, then puts it on mine. And if it's a test, I don't care. I don't pull my hand away. I let her touch me freely in this bar where no one knows me, anyway. But, at this stage, even if someone did, I wouldn't care. I wouldn't. "Come on," she says, and I'd follow her to the end of the earth.

Outside, it's chilly for the time of year—or not, because this is late summer in London. And outside the cosy cocoon of the bar where Joy's face was all I saw, her words were all I heard, I find myself teetering more towards the edge of where my desire and my common sense meet. I feel myself becoming a rationally thinking human being again, but I still follow her quick strides on the pavement and have her take me home. And this, more than anything, this mixture of judgement clouded by infatuation—or 'being horny' as Joy would surely call it—but still being well aware of what I'm doing, of not being able to plead temporary insanity, is what will get me through her door.

Joy's flat is quirky but big for London—or perhaps it's different in this new-to-me area—but I truly have no interest in appraising her interior design skills. She's the most beautiful part of it, as she lets her leather jacket carelessly slip from her shoulders and throws it over the armrest of the sofa. She eyes me for a few long, silent seconds as I just stand there, probably looking forlorn, but actually wrapped up in a lust so all-consuming, I can barely move. Never in my life, not at any moment in time—neither in Portugal, nor when I was younger—have I wanted someone more than I want Joy now. Because I'm familiar with her body already, and I know what she can do to me, and I just want more and more. More of the same, but with different variations perhaps. It doesn't even matter, I just want to be with her. So, I don't wait for her to come for me. My lips part, I take the few steps that separate us and bring my hands behind her neck to pull her close.

"I've missed you too," I say, at last. I should have said it last night, but then the other Alice was still in charge.

"I can tell," Joy says. "Oh, how I can tell." And I don't know if she's referring to the state I'm in now, or if I gave myself away so easily last night. It doesn't matter. All that matters are her lips on mine, her tongue darting into my mouth, her hands in my hair, tugging at my clothes, unzipping the pair of jeans I never wear but thought I should wear today, for this date. For this trial. "If you still feel the same way after that, I'll walk away," Joy said last night and the very thought of her doing so feels like a punch to the gut.

"Am I a dirty old woman now?" I asked Joy in Portugal. By then I knew to expect a snarky response, but she surprised me.

"You're not old, Alice. And there's nothing dirty about what we're doing. It's all in your head."

Here and now, in Joy's flat, I don't feel old or dirty. I feel alive, as if injected with a brand new life force. I feel twenty years younger than my driver's license says. And I just let go, I let myself be carried by the wave of lust that rides through my veins, by the energy I get back from Joy when we kiss and kiss, and become naked in a matter of minutes. And it's frantic how we jumble towards her bedroom, and topple onto the bed, but at least we make it there before I fall apart completely. Only streetlight illuminates the room, but when I open my eyes for more than a fraction in between wild, lustful kisses, I notice a mirror to my right, one to my left, and one in front of me as well. Before I can even think 'good grief' or 'what on earth?' Joy is on top of me, her legs spread wide, her hot, hot sex on my stomach. I haven't seen her naked, beautiful breasts for far too long, I think instead, and grab them, gently at first, but from the very second we set foot in this flat, we both knew this is not a time for gentleness—this is a time for taking, for stealing from one another what we both so desperately, so achingly need.

Joy throws her head back, exposing her neck, as I knead her breasts, roll her nipples between my fingers, until I bring a hand down and think, yes, I want to see her come like this. I want her to sit on top of me, and I want to examine every inch of her I'm able to see in the semi-darkness of her room, the traffic swishing outside, bouts of laughter rising up to the first-floor window.

But, before my finger even makes it all the way down, I feel Joy's hand on my inner thigh, her fingers crawling closer. With her arm behind her, she leans her body to her right—the hand with which she's going to fuck me.

My finger is on her clitoris now, circling around, feeling her wetness, slipping inside only the littlest bit, until I can't stop myself any longer and the urge to be inside her is too big. And the very act of entering her, of feeling her there, of reaching this pinnacle of intimacy, coincides—although I'm sure it's not a coincidence—with her finger reaching my clitoris, and I'm on fire. My blood has caught fire and my skin is burning and all oxygen is being drained from my lungs. I try to keep my eyes open, try to take in the sensual bucking of her body, the swaying of her breasts, the ripple of her belly. But then she slips her finger inside me as deep as she can in the position she's in, slides it out, and rubs my clitoris with the copious wetness she has found in me. She repeats this, again and again, and my eyes fall shut in a growing sensation of ecstasy, and I keep thrusting my own fingers into her, searching for that spot that I already know drives her crazy.

The explosion is soft and hard at the same time, warm and liquid, demanding, obliterating.

"Oh Christ," I holler, not caring how loud. Joy said in Quinta that the volume of my moans increased with the number of orgasms I've had. "Keep this up and you'll be breaking the sound barrier soon," she joked. But this is years of denied pleasure burrowing its way out of me, more than a decade of being untouched. This was never going to be silent once I allowed myself to really let go. "Oh God, Joy."

When I come to, my fingers are still buried inside her, but Joy's hands are in her hair now, her breasts jutting out, and she's riding me, taking control, her breathing coming quicker, and I give her everything I have. I give her my love, my doubts, my trepidations, my insecurities. I channel it all in what I'm doing to her. Lay myself bare for her while I look at her body surrendering and I've never seen anything more beautiful in my life. And, in that moment, I know with dead certainty, that I will not walk away. To do so would be to deny myself life itself. This new life she has given me. I'm not going back to the old Alice McAllister. I couldn't if I tried.

When orgasm shudders through her, and the sight of it floors me so much a tear wells in the corner of my eye, I know I'm hers. She's got me. She played and won. Not that I consider myself the losing party at all.

CHAPTER FIFTEEN

When I wake up the next morning the first thing I see is my own reflection in one of Joy's mirrors. The woman I see is me, undoubtedly so, but something has changed. She's in love, I think. This is me completely infatuated with someone twenty-two years younger than me.

I turn to look at Joy, and my shifting in the bed must have woken her, because she opens her eyes and, instantly, a smile transforms her sleepy face into one of wonder and pleasure and, I guess, love.

"Why so many mirrors?" I ask, my hand finding hers under the sheet.

"Trust me, Alice," Joy says, her voice still croaky from just waking up, "it's only a matter of time before you fully understand."

"What does that mean—" I ask, but Joy has shuffled towards me and kisses me on the mouth.

"Good morning, Cougar," she whispers in between kisses. "You made me miss dinner last night and I'm positively starving."

"Do you have anything in your fridge that can serve as breakfast?"

"No." Joy hoists herself on top of me, reviving images of last night. "But I have you." She slinks her body down mine, her hard nipples drawing a straight line down my belly, then my legs.

Is she really going to do what I think she's going to do? After all we did last night? Is her hunger for me really so great?

Joy throws the sheets off us, and the air against my skin makes me break out in goosebumps. She kisses the line of skin above my pubic hair, then makes her way down, and I wonder if there's a limit to this. If there's such a thing as a given number of climaxes in twenty-four hours that the human body can't exceed without consequences. But then Joy pushes my legs apart, and I draw up my knees, and her breath is on my sex—I don't think I'll ever get used to the word pussy—and then her tongue touches me, and then I'm lost. When I thrash my head to the left in pleasure, I catch a glimpse of myself in the mirror. My first instinct is to look away, to not want to see myself like that, but the reflection is strangely compelling and, I must admit, arousing. Joy's tongue slips in and out of me, and flicks along my clitoris, along my pulsing lips and I keep staring at myself in the mirror. At the transformation on my face, the bewilderment in my eyes, at how my body meets her movements with its own, accommodates her.

As Joy brings me closer, my eyes narrow, but I don't close them because, by now, I want to see. I want to see what she sees when I come. I want to know the secret. And what I see is a woman who is writhing and groaning at an ever-increasing pace, and whose face contorts as if in agony, while actually she's in the midst of, she has recently learned, one of life's greatest pleasures.

Despite my desire to see, the world goes black for a few instants as a hot glow passes through my body, and I've given myself up to her once again, shown my truest self, and I cry out, I guess, louder than any of the times I did last night.

"Now we can go for breakfast," Joy says after she has crawled back up my body the way she slithered down earlier, before my world shifted in her direction a little more again. If it keeps changing, if I keep coming unstuck from who I used to be, I wonder where I will end up?

"You have to give me a few minutes to recover. I am

middle-aged, remember?" I snicker at my own silly joke, more to ignore the truth of it than because it's funny.

"Alice." No one has ever let my name slip from their lips the way Joy has, I think. "Take all the time you need."

Time, I think suddenly. It's Sunday. I have to go to work tomorrow and face Miranda. Whatever will I say when she asks how my weekend was?

To distract myself from the encroaching despair of having to face reality, I ask, "Do you really not have any breakfast ingredients or were you just saying that?" I have turned on my side, certain body parts still throbbing, so past feeling any qualms about being naked with another person, it doesn't fail to astound me once again.

"I may have an egg or two. I'm not sure." She kisses me on the tip of my nose and I can smell myself on her lips. "But I'm seriously starving, and they do a marvellous Sunday brunch just around the corner."

"Is that, er, a good idea?" I ask. "Should we maybe go to another neighbourhood instead? Somewhere nobody knows you?"

"We could…" Joy's voice trails off as she ponders. "But fuck, if I don't eat something within the next half hour I may die of starvation. I'm not kidding, Alice. You've depleted me of all my energy. I'll barely make it into the shower, but I really do think I owe it to our fellow restaurant goers to wash the hours of sex we had off me." She shoots me one of her smiles. "I know you're worried, but at this hour of the day, it's highly unlikely we'll bump into anyone familiar and, well, if we're going to do this we can't always go to Enfield or Bromley."

"Are we then?" I ask. "Doing… this?" The answer is so blindingly clear it makes my question obsolete, but still, some things need to be said out loud a few times before they can actually begin to make sense.

"You tell me, Alice?" I feel her breath run across my cheeks as she speaks. "Do you want to go back to pretending

I don't exist? Or did I make enough of a case to make you try?"

"The case you made was unusually devoid of words and extremely tactile." I trace my finger along her arm, unable to resist touching her.

"I'm in love with you, Alice. I want to go out with you. I want to know everything about you. I want to wake up next to you as many times as I can. And, by God, I want to fuck you. I want to see you come alive like that time and time again." She kisses my nose again. "Is that enough of a case?"

"It is." I let myself fall onto my back and stare into her eyes. "I have no counterarguments."

"Then will you go to breakfast with me?"

I nod and pull her closer again, because keeping my distance has, overnight, become a thing of the past.

★ ★ ★

Joy orders a double omelette with two slices of toast, a fruit salad, a bowl of yoghurt and a glass of champagne for breakfast. I'm hungry, but also nervous, so I limit myself to a cup of black coffee and a croissant.

"The decreasing need for food should only start after seventy, you know," Joy says after the waiter has taken our order, and I wonder if he was thinking, *how lovely, a mother and daughter on a brunch date.* "Relax, Alice. Just breathe. It's no fun when you're uptight like that."

"You're not the one who has a daily staff meeting with Miranda on top of two big client meetings the upcoming week. So give me a break, please."

"We can sit here and compare grief over this all day long. It's not going to change anything. The only thing that will need to change if we want this—and I think we've established that we do—is you and your perspective."

"I'm sorry, Joy. I feel so ill at ease. I feel so… gawked at. I mean, people may assume I'm your mother, but that actually makes it even worse."

Joy extends her arm over the table and reaches for my hand just as the waiter brings our beverages. While he deposits my cup and her glass on the table, she strokes the top of my hand with her thumb. "There," she says, once the waiter has retreated, "now at least one person in this establishment won't think of you as my mother anymore."

Whereas I had expected her touch to jolt me, to make me feel on display even more, it has a calming effect on my frayed nerves. "I'm going to need some time to adjust to this." I squeeze her fingers between mine, not wanting her to retract her hand.

"As I said, you have all the time in the world." With her other hand, she lifts her champagne glass and takes a quick sip. "Ah, brunch was invented to drink champagne before lunch, you know, but I digress." Her thumb is still stroking my skin. "I'm not a teenager, Alice. My father died when I was fifteen. I went off to college in the States on my own when I was eighteen. I've seen a thing or two. I'm not some naive, spoiled brat. This is entirely a two-way street and, well, fuck what anyone else thinks. I've told you before, I truly don't care."

"Why *did* you go to college in LA?"

"Because no reputable university in the UK would take me." She chuckles, then shrugs. "I just wanted a change, wanted to get away… wanted a place away from home to discover myself. And perhaps it was also an act of rebellion against Mum and Jeff." She sips again. "I don't know. There's no clearly defined reason. It's just something I wanted to do. And I've never regretted it."

"So… when you were in LA discovering yourself…" It's as if Joy can so easily read me, as if she has a clear view into my brain and can follow my train of thought. She's smiling already. Somehow, she knows what's coming. It's a question I had wanted to ask her back in Portugal but I wasn't yet able to work up the nerve. "How many, er, people did you, huh, discover yourself with?"

"Good grief, Alice, you are so bloody adorable when you get all flustered like that." She removes her hand and leans back in her seat, regarding me while she makes a show of counting on her fingers. "So you want to know how many women I slept with before you, right?" She shrugs again. "It's a fair enough question. No need to get your knickers in a twist about it."

"Oh Christ, I wish I'd never asked." Joy doesn't annoy me when she's coy with me like this, when she toys with my emotions and my boundaries. Her wit and mild sarcasm amuse and delight me.

"I'd say… eight and a half." She nods. "Yes, that's my final number."

"Eight and a half?" It's my turn to give her a faux-mocking smile. "Do explain."

"Well, there was this girl called Ellen who I felt up at a party once, but then we got distracted, I guess, and we didn't actually consummate. I can't discount her, but I can't really count her either."

I'm astounded once again by how completely different Joy's coming-of-age process was from mine. Alan was my first and, up until a month ago, my last.

"Do tell me more," I say, and while we eat our breakfast—Joy taking giant bites of omelette and occasionally speaking with her mouth full—she takes me through the stories of the first girl she was with, the first one who really broke her heart, the one she almost stayed in the US for, and all the ones in between. "Of all of them, only two were pure one-night stands, but I quickly figured out that's not really my thing," she says. And later, "Alex and I fucked for the first time in her office."

I love hearing her talk, love how easy she is with divulging all this personal information and I don't even mind the complete lack of discretion she displays because I can see that this is how she is. A girl with her heart on her sleeve. I listen to her with ever-growing amazement, and every time she uses the completely unnecessary word *fuck*, be it as a verb or just as an expletive, my ears burn.

"Were you in love with Alex?" I ask, because I may as well know it all now. My question gives her pause, though, and I guess that says enough.

"It was difficult. I mean, I surely had feelings for her, but it's hard to really see them for what they were. Were they more intense because of the thrill of sleeping with my boss?" She lifts her shoulders. "It could be. But, most of all, it was pure madness. Now *that* was sneaking around. No one in the office could find out, because, well, that workplace was not the sort of place where things like that happened, let alone were condoned. She was my superior, but not the big chief, you know? She had people to answer to as well. It was just messy, I guess. Irresponsible." Joy's tone has changed. She sounds less excited, more sedate—perhaps it's all the food she jammed down her throat in record time.

"Does she still text you?" I remember the messages she received on the night we first kissed in Portugal, when she made a point of switching her phone off.

"Only when she's drunk." Joy's gaze drifts to her phone, which she always keeps somewhere in sight. "Do I detect a hint of jealousy in your line of questioning?"

"No," I say, despite a merciless blush creeping from my neck to my cheeks. "I'm just curious."

"Again, nothing wrong with that." She winks at me, and paints that grin on her face again, and I feel it all the way to my core.

"How about we go for a stroll and walk off all this food?" she asks.

We settle the bill and make our way out to the street. There she takes my hand in hers and we meander through her neighbourhood like that. Joy points out some interesting bars and restaurants, and once I've got used to the sensation of walking down the street hand-in-hand with someone else, and lean into her a bit, just because I can, an unexpected sense of freedom settles in me. A sense that with Joy by my side, I can do anything.

CHAPTER SIXTEEN

Three weeks go by during which the balance of my life shifts from *work, home, sleep* to *work, Joy, sleep together*. We find a rhythm: Joy comes to my place once or twice during the week and I stay at hers over the weekend. It's a rhythm that suits me and allows me to process the changes in my life, and in myself, as gradually as possible. The weather changes abruptly from late summer to autumn, and we spend most of our time indoors, hidden away from everyone.

During work hours, my ever-growing guilt stands in stark contrast to the giddiness I feel when I'm with Joy: the ease of it all, the sexiness, and how she can play my body as though she hasn't done anything else in her adult life. I almost sigh with relief when Miranda tells me she's going to Paris for a long weekend with Jeff. Because whenever I see her, and I see Miranda all the time, the nagging voice in my head reminds me of all the acts I engage in with her daughter. Also, there's the realisation that I'm deceiving her, that the longer this goes on without her knowing, the bigger the damage will be.

Yet, the mere notion of telling her is completely inconceivable. On Fridays after work I usually need at least half of bottle of wine to calm my nerves. I'm always so tense after a week of coping with my workload, and now, on top of that is the voice of guilt, and, increasingly, the shame.

But what Joy and I have is more powerful than any shame and, when I'm with her, I don't feel the slightest twinge of it. While we do go out for meals and we went to see a movie together once, I also realise that our relationship is not lived in the real world. The realm of our affair is her flat, my house, and a handful of restaurants. I don't tell anyone about her and every time she asks me if I would, perhaps, like to meet one of her friends, like her best friend Marcy, who is starting to wonder what the hell is going on with her, I reply, "Not yet."

"I'm not asking you to come out to Mum, Alice," Joy says on the Friday that Miranda leaves for Paris. "I just, I don't know, want to integrate you—us—into my life more. I'm the opposite of a hermit. Keep me inside for too long and I'll go mad. Besides, I'm proud to be seen with you. I want you to meet my friends."

"Please, feel free to go out as much as you like. You don't have to stay in because of me."

"I'm not saying we should go clubbing or anything. I could just have some friends over and introduce you. They're a very diverse group. I'm sure you'll like them."

And, perhaps because Miranda is out of town, I'm more amenable to the idea than I would otherwise be. "Okay," I say. "We can do that."

"We can?" Joy's eyes grow wide with excitement.

"Well, yes, like you said, we can't pretend there's no outside world forever. Just be sure you can trust them. I don't want this reaching Miranda's ears."

"Not to worry. All my friends are very trustworthy." We are at Joy's flat in Shoreditch, sitting with our legs intertwined, playing with each other's fingers while just talking the way we have grown accustomed to. It has only taken three weeks to make the thought of going home to my own empty house on a Friday evening completely unbearable. "But, Alice, my feelings for you are hardly diminishing and we're going to have to come clean to Mum sooner rather than later."

"I know, but first things first. Let's start by seeing how your friends feel about me. Then, we'll take it from there. Who are you inviting?"

"Marcy and Ben, for sure. And perhaps Justin and Bobby, although they can be bit crass."

"More crass than you?"

"Compared to them, I speak like Princess Anne." She chuckles and runs a hand through her hair.

✷ ✷ ✷

Joy has invited five of her friends for afternoon tea that Sunday. For this occasion, she has amazed me once again and baked two cakes the day before—while I looked on in bewilderment. To my surprise, when we went to Tesco after breakfast, she also insisted on hauling six bottles of Prosecco back to her flat.

"But it's afternoon tea," I argued.

"That's exactly right, Alice," was all Joy had to say to that, and I was, once again, left to conclude that most of Joy's social activities come with a serious tipple.

My alcohol intake has surely increased since I started seeing Joy, but I've always made a point of not drinking more than one glass of wine on Sunday—Mondays are hard enough these days without a hangover. I used to love Mondays, that exciting buzz of a new week, of going to the firm that Miranda and I built from nothing. But nowadays a lot of these sentiments are drowned out by guilt, and, in my head at least, my Monday morning entrance into the office has transformed into a walk of shame.

By three, all of Joy's friends have arrived and it becomes clear that her flat is actually not as big as I always thought it was. Marcy and Ben are parked on the sofa—the same one on which she gave me a shuddering climax only the evening before—and Justin and Bobby, two men closer in age to me than to Joy, each perch on an armrest, while Mindy, a former colleague from the job Joy left because of Alex, hangs—rather uncomfortably from the look of it—in a bean bag. Joy and I dispense drinks. By then, I'm not at all surprised that no one is drinking actual tea.

"Alice," says Justin, who hasn't kept his mouth shut for

one single second since arriving, "I am so glad to meet you. It was so obvious Joy was seeing someone. I was about to call her out on it, but she just beat me to it with this invitation." He lifts his glass. "Here's to you."

I smile at him bashfully. At first, I thought I'd carry myself the way I do when I meet new clients, but that resolution flew out of the window when this motley crew walked in. A professional manner has no place here. Then, I *am* grateful for the alcohol Joy has provided. I need some social lubricant right about now.

I'm not sure what Joy has said to them exactly, or if she has divulged any details about how we met, but she must have said something, because nobody asks me about it. They are nice people and much more courteous than Joy made them out to be, and once they have politely grilled me on my profession—"nice!"—and where I live—"ooh, fancy!"—they talk amongst themselves in the way that people who've known each other for a while do. Nobody even hints at Miranda's existence, which makes me feel safe, and allows me to linger in my illusion a while longer. As far as steps into the world together with Joy go, this first one is much easier than I had feared.

Joy's six bottles of bubbles run out very quickly, but of course they've all brought bottles as a gift, and I grow ever more amazed at how much these people can drink. Joy, especially, I notice is knocking back glass after glass. She must have been nervous about this as well and I can't hold it against her that she's letting her hair down.

"Hey, Joy," Bobby asks when everyone is more than merry. "Do you have any of that stuff from Diego left?"

"Ooh," Justin coos, and he almost claps his hands. "Yes, please."

I see Joy stiffen, but only a fraction. She must have drunk more than a bottle all by herself by now. "Sure, but I'm not rolling," she says. "It's in that drawer just behind you, Jus."

Before I even realise what's going on and my mind computes that they're referring to drugs, Justin produces a bag of marijuana from the cabinet that Joy mentioned.

I look at Joy in a panic, hoping to telegraph to her that I'm not okay with this. I'm a lawyer, and cannabis is still illegal in the UK. This is absolutely not something I want to be a part of. But Joy doesn't look at me; instead she gazes in front of her, her eyes glassy from too much alcohol.

"I'll do the honours," Mindy volunteers, and positions herself at the coffee table which carries remnants of Joy's two cakes.

Without saying anything, I get up, pick up the two trays and carry them to the kitchen, hoping that Joy will follow me so that I can explain to her that I don't want to be a part of this, but nobody follows me into the kitchen. I pour myself a glass of water and assess my options. On Sunday evening I usually go back to my house anyway, so I'll just head home.

"I think this is my cue to leave," I announce when I'm back in the living room.

"What? Alice, no!" Justin says. "Are you not cool with this? I'm sorry, I should have asked you first."

"That's perfectly fine. You should all do what you want to do. I have an early day tomorrow, anyway." It's not even seven and still light outside. But I suddenly feel so ridiculous, so out of place, so completely and utterly out of my depth, that I just want to run away, no matter how silly and old and goody-two-shoes fleeing the scene makes me look.

"Come on, Alice," Joy says, but doesn't get up, "it's just a joint. It's really no big deal." From the way she looks at me I can tell that it's hurting her that I'm about to leave.

"Then let it be no big deal to all of you without me and enjoy," I say, with a bitterness to my tone that surprises me. But it's as though the huge sand castle of illusion I have built in the past few weeks is crumbling so fast, I have to hurry if I want to make it out alive. "It was lovely meeting all of you. Really," I say to the group. "I'll call you later," I say to Joy, who still doesn't get up.

Without gathering any of my belongings except my purse, I fetch my jacket from the hallway and hurry out of the door. Once I've shut it behind me, I take a deep breath, and make my way down the stairs, somewhat hoping Joy will come after me but mostly hoping she won't. She's too inebriated to reason with now, anyway, I tell myself, when no one follows me. Within seconds, I'm standing outside Joy's building.

It wasn't the age difference between Joy's friends and me—Bobby is mid forties, Justin a bit younger—or their conversation, too hip and in-the-know for me to follow or engage in, that urged me to escape the scene. It wasn't even so much that they were about to roll a joint and share it, I assume, convivially. It's how far removed I felt from Joy. From who she is when she's not with me: someone who drinks too much, and smokes marijuana. But more than that, someone who, clearly, didn't care about the distress I was feeling in that moment. And the thing is that I don't even blame her. It's not Joy's duty to stop having a good time on a wonderful Sunday afternoon with her friends because her 'girlfriend'—God, that word and the ways in which it doesn't apply to me—is upset. Nor is it her friends' duty to not mention Joy's mother at all, no matter how well they can act as though Miranda doesn't exist and there's no connection between us.

★ ★ ★

When I get home and look at my reflection in the mirror, which now always makes me think of Joy's bedroom mirrors, I say to myself, my voice dripping with sarcasm and sadness, "Welcome back, Alice."

CHAPTER SEVENTEEN

As agreed before she left for Paris, Miranda only arrives at work around lunch time the next Monday. The very first time she went on one of those weekends, a few years after we'd founded the firm, I had told her, "If only you had the same work ethic as I. This firm could be so successful."

Miranda, with her usual snark, a quality I've often vocally lamented but appreciate in her nonetheless—and recognise so much of in Joy—said, "I didn't become my own boss to listen to my business partner boss me around, Alice. If you want to work eighty hours a week, be my guest, but me? I have a life to live. A life outside these office walls. I do wish you'd do the same."

Today, I'm grateful for the different ways in which we lead our lives. Throughout the morning, though, I seem to have picked up one of Joy's habits: I can't keep my eyes off my phone. After I got home last night, I broke my promise to Joy and didn't call her because I failed to see the point. What would I have said to her while she was drunk *and* stoned? Yet, I found myself sleeping only the lightest, most fitful of sleeps, my ears perked to catch the smallest noise. Someone at my front door, perhaps. Or, at the very least, the beep of my phone. Unfortunately, it was one of the most silent nights of my life, the silence only punctured by the desperate sighs coming from my mouth and my restless body writhing against the freshly ironed sheets.

It's only when Miranda knocks on the door of my office, just at the very moment she peeks her head inside, that my phone finally releases me from my agony. I reach for it, but can't read the message while I'm talking to Miranda.

"How was your trip?" I ask.

"Wonderful as usual," Miranda says. "Excellent food, great wine, and the most beautiful city in the world. What more can I ask for?" Her gaze rests on me for longer than it usually would. "Can I come in for a second or are you in the middle of something?"

My eyes wander to my phone, but I push it away. "Of course." I nod for her to sit.

"Don't take this the wrong way, Alice, but that super-healthy complexion you brought back from Portugal has vanished completely and seems to have been replaced by something else… Are you all right? There's isn't anything… medical going on, is there?"

"No, no, I'm perfectly fine," I'm quick to say—perhaps too quick.

"You've been different since you came back. More easily distracted, I guess. And, well, today you just look so un-Alice-like. Is it something else? Something I can help with?"

"My dinner disagreed with me and I didn't sleep very well last night, that's all." I suddenly feel very self-conscious about my appearance. Is my lack of sleep so visible? Or is Miranda so apt at spotting it because we have, after all, known each other for most of our adult lives. And if she can so easily see this, what else does she see?

"Yeah? Are you sure? I'm—" My phone beeps again, repeating the new message alert. I never managed to switch of that annoying function. Miranda continues undeterred. "I'm worried about you, that's all."

"I'm fine. I promise you." Ridiculously, I hold up my hand the way a girl scout would. "Just a few rough days, and this weather isn't helping."

"I'm always here for you if there's anything at all you want to talk about," Miranda says with great earnest. She must be really worried about me. While I appreciate her concern, I can only sigh inwardly at the impossibility of this entire situation. I could also use a conversation with my best friend right about now.

"Thank you, Miranda. I appreciate that." Inadvertently, I stare at my phone again. I have no idea how I can even keep a straight face. I'm so unfamiliar with this sort of emotional distress.

"I'll let you get that," she says.

Shame rises from somewhere deep in my gut, translating into a fierce and sudden blush on my cheeks. Luckily, Miranda is already turning to leave.

"Don't work so hard, Alice. Really, I know you enjoy your job, and so do I, but it's not worth it in the end. It never is."

"I'll go to bed early tonight," I say to her back as she exits my office. As soon as I see her round the corner, I read the message on my phone.

Sorry, is all it says.

Sorry? That's it. What am I supposed to do with that? I'm guessing not even youth is a good enough cure for the hangover Joy must be suffering today—the physical *and* the emotional one.

I type back: *I'm sorry too. I hope you understand why I couldn't stay.*

Early on, we agreed to not text each other while at work, and I feel increasingly ill at ease as our text message conversation continues. But I certainly can't call her when Miranda could walk back through my door at any second. I put a stop to the texting back and forth—which is something I never did before I met Joy—and invite her to my house to talk after work.

While I eat a quick sandwich at my desk, I question Google about ways to conceal dark circles under one's eyes and other obvious signs of fatigue and distress.

★ ★ ★

Because I presume Joy will be hungry, I buy ingredients for a salad so I can serve her dinner when she arrives. By the time I reach my house, she's already there, her backside perched on the steps in front of my door.

"I hope you haven't waited too long?" I ask, awkwardly.

"Fuck, Alice," she says. "What are we doing?"

This is it, I think, she has reached the same conclusion as I have. The supreme thrill of the first few weeks is starting to wear off, and we are left with the cold hard facts of our situation: no matter how you twist or turn it, it's impossible.

"Let's go inside." I quickly let us in, ignoring the knot coiling in my stomach. Because, really, all I want to do is take her in my arms and tell her everything's going to be okay. To kiss that frown from her face, to bury my nose in her hair. But it would just be more lies, more fooling ourselves. "Do you want something to eat?" I ask when we've reached the kitchen.

"Alice, please." Joy reaches for my arm, curls her fingers around my wrist. "Listen to me. I'm not someone who hides what I feel. I'm sorry about, er, letting go so much last night. I was blowing off steam, you know? This whole situation has been stressful for me too. I'm close to my mum and I'm finally at a stage where I could actually tell her about the new person I'm seeing, but instead, every time we talk, I can't say anything at all. I feel like I'm going back into the closet and it's killing me."

"I understand. I feel the same way." We're both still wearing our coats. It stands in such stark contrast to how naked we were when we first met, as though we've had to add layer after layer to survive our lives after coming back from Portugal. The knot in my stomach seems to be making its way up to my throat, lodging itself there. "I know there's only one solution." While I know this needs to end, I also know it's going to hurt me in ways I've never been hurt before—not even when Alan left. To have to kill something that's so glorious, that feels so good, that's still in such an early stage it's still brimming with vibrancy and possibilities, is so hard, I don't even know how to say the words.

"We have to tell Mum," Joy says. "If we want to stand any chance at all, we have to tell her, because if we don't, it's going to eat us alive. It's going to be the end of us before we've even begun."

"W-what?" I stammer. Because this was decidedly not the solution I had in mind. "No. I don't agree. I don't."

"What do you mean you don't agree? You just said you did. You said you knew there was only one solution. I mean, apart from running away, there is really only one way to go about this." As she says this, I see how the moment of realisation comes and transforms her face into something so devastating I almost need to look away. "Oh fuck, no, Alice. I'm not breaking up with you. I'm not even having that conversation again. We've made our decision. Nu-uh."

"Miranda will not accept it. I will lose her. I will lose my best friend and business partner. She may very well decide to leave the firm because of this."

"Oh, so it's a choice between me and my mum now, is it?" I see the fight rise in Joy, see how her muscles tense and she straightens her spine. "Well, I dare you to walk away from this. Let's see how fucking miserable that's going to make you."

"Don't you see how impossible this is for me?" I plead.

"She's my mother, Alice. I am her flesh and blood. If I'm willing to stand up for us, for this beautiful thing that is growing between us, then why can't you?"

"I don't know. Because I'm a coward. Because I don't want to be *that* person to Miranda."

"And what person would that be? The woman who makes her daughter happy? If you take away your fear, there's not a lot left of your reasoning, if only you could see that."

"*My* fear? How about *your* naïveté? Do you really think Miranda is going to accept us being together because she wants you to be happy?" I shake my head in defeat. "I think your reasoning is much more flawed than mine."

"Look, I know you're scared." Joy injects some unexpected tenderness into her tone. "And overwhelmed and probably feeling just as crazy as I am right now. But, Alice, you must understand, I'm not letting you go. The way you've made me feel since I arrived in Quinta is so much more powerful than anything I've ever felt for any other woman. We have something special and, I guess, if you can't see that and if you don't feel the same way, then yes, that's a reason to end it, but I know you feel it too. It's plain as day. Can you honestly stand here and tell me that you aren't crazy, madly in love with me?"

"No." It's all I can say at first when confronted with Joy in most excellent arguer mode. "But you seem to adhere to this foolish notion that love can overcome anything. Let me tell you here and now that it can't."

"Oh really? And how would you know, Alice? Are you the big expert on love all of a sudden?" As soon as she says it, something changes about Joy's demeanour. She steps closer and looks into my eyes. "I'm sorry. I shouldn't have said that. I was just lashing out. Can we take a step back? Take off our coats, perhaps, and sit down?"

"Okay." I take a deep breath and turn to get a glass of water. I hear Joy shrug off her coat. While I drink to calm myself down, I think about all the things I can't say to her: what if it doesn't work out? What if the age difference, and all our other differences, prove too big a hurdle in the end? What if we tell Miranda and months later you meet someone younger, someone more suitable, and I will have lost it all?

We both take a seat at the kitchen table and I offer Joy some water as well.

"Alice," she takes my hand in hers, "in your head you've already played out the worst case scenario. I can absolutely guarantee you that it won't be as bad as you think. There's just no way. Mum cares about you too. She always speaks highly of you. You have done so much for her over the years. She wants nothing more than for you to be happy as well. I'm not claiming she will embrace you as my partner from the get-go. She will need to adjust to the idea. But while she does, we can prove to her that being with each other makes us happier than we've ever been. I know you need to take a leap of faith in order to go through with this, and I know that takes a lot, but you're not doing this alone, Alice. We're doing this together." Joy sits back, presumably to examine the effects of another excellently made case.

"In theory, your arguments make sense, but, I... I just don't see it. I can't even think about it, truth be told."

"Don't you want to have tried, though? For us? Do you really think you can live with the regret if you don't?"

I shake my head. "I don't know. I really don't know. There's this war waging within me. I've always been a very rational person, very reasonable and logical, and all the logic I have accumulated over the years assures me that telling Miranda is the worst possible thing I can do. But then, there's this other side of me, a side I haven't been in touch with for so long—if ever. And my emotional side tells me that, yes, I need to do this. That I owe it to you: for what you have done for me, to how you've brought me out of my shell and made a whole new woman out of me. It's just so, so hard."

"I know, sweetheart, I know." Joy shuffles closer, chair and all and puts her hands on my knees. When was the last time someone called me by a term of endearment? I have no recollection. And, of course, when I'm with Joy, emotion *will* win. But I can't strap Joy to my side to carry her around with me through my everyday life. She won't be there when I go into the office day after day to face Miranda's condemning stare. "But we have to tell her. We have no choice."

As Joy digs her fingers into my thigh, I realise we could argue back and forth all night. Mull over the pros and cons until dawn breaks, but it won't change anything in the end.

There is no easy outcome, no quick fix, and, when it comes down to it, I will still have a choice to make. Head or heart. Love or friendship. Give in to fear or stand up for what Joy and I have.

"Okay," I hear myself say after a few minutes of silence. A few minutes during which I imagine asking Joy to leave and not contact me again. A few minutes during which I realise that, despite it being the hardest thing I'll ever do, the choice was made for me that night when Joy kissed me and nothing was ever the same again. My fear is me clinging onto the old Alice, the always-careful workaholic who had given up on love completely. The person I see less and less of when I look in the mirror. The person I no longer deserve to be. "Let's do it." The determination in my voice surprises even me.

CHAPTER EIGHTEEN

"See you at eight," Miranda says on Friday and as I see her walk out of the office I can't help but think it's the end of an era. After tonight, my friendship with Miranda will be forever changed. Joy and I have talked a lot in the past week about the best way to go about telling her. "Let's just go to Mum's house now," she said on Wednesday evening. "Let's just get it over with." Of course, I disagreed. Instead, I asked Joy to find out what she was doing the next weekend, and if there was a possible time when we could tell just her. Somehow, the thought of having to confess to Jeff as well made it all even more unbearable.

So, tonight's the night. Miranda and Joy are coming to dinner at my house, while Jeff is out of town at a, as Joy called it, 'douchebag seminar' in Brighton. Miranda was more than keen to accept my invitation and didn't question me when I asked her to extend it to Joy as well.

"I'm not sure she'll be able to make it," Miranda did say, "I think she's seeing someone but I'm doing my very best not to be pushy about it. She'll tell me when she's ready."

Part of my decency died when I replied, wearing my best poker face, "I'm sure she will."

Because what we're about to do to Miranda is not fair in any way, shape or form. Her life will change as well. Her perception of her daughter and her best friend will be altered forever in the course of one evening, one conversation.

I leave work as soon as Miranda has exited the building

to make sure my house is spotless. To avoid the risk of serving Miranda a non-stellar meal on a night like this I ordered a roast chicken and gratin potatoes from a deli in my street. I polish the wine glasses until they sparkle. Check myself in the mirror a dozen times and, every time, I'm able to look back less and less. Joy arrives at seven-thirty and she hugs me for a long time. First, I offered the plan of telling Miranda by myself, arguing that, perhaps, she would be able to better accept it if she didn't have to look at the both of us while she processed the news, but Joy wouldn't have any of that.

"We do this together," she said, and I couldn't argue with her.

We pace around the house as though we've taken some nervous energy drug until the chime of the doorbell announces it's show time. This is it. I inhale deeply and open the door to Miranda. She has brought a bunch of gorgeous dahlias and a bottle of wine, because Miranda is the kind of person who can not be invited somewhere and not bring two courtesy gifts at the very least.

"This is so nice of you, Alice," she says. "I do hope a new tradition is born." She walks into the living room and hugs her daughter. "I feel like I never see you anymore. You do still live in London, don't you?" she asks Joy playfully. "Or do they work you too hard at your new job?"

I serve nibbles and red wine while we chit-chat in the lounge. After much debate, Joy and I agreed to tell her after we've eaten.

"Why not just tell her as soon as we sit down?" Joy asked. "I'm not sure I can hold my nerve for so long. We will have to pretend we're just acquaintances, Alice. Do you know how hard that is?"

"It's nothing compared to actually telling her," I replied, which shut Joy up quickly.

I can tell how nervous Joy is, though, by how she chatters ceaselessly. About the guy she sits across from at work and how his beard is untrimmed and gross and so passé, and how Marcy and Ben are trying to get pregnant but have had no luck just yet, and how a friend named Rupert she has mentioned a few times to me has come out at work and on and on.

If she keeps this up, Miranda will grow suspicious very quickly, I think. But Miranda just seems to enjoy being in her daughter's company and then I'm about to conclude that maybe this is how they are together—Joy talking, Miranda listening—when it dawns on me that we've finished our meal and I rise to clear the plates.

"I'll help you," Joy says, and we both grab Miranda's plate at the same time, our combined nervousness filling the room, and we both let go at the same time as well, leaving Miranda with a puzzled look on her face.

After we clear the table and I've poured Miranda a generous helping of wine, I look at Joy and nod. We've agreed that she'll do the actual talking and I'll jump in when needed and try to answer the questions that Miranda will surely have.

"Mum, I, er, we, have something to tell you."

I can't look at Miranda so I focus my gaze on a spot on the wall behind her.

"You do?" From the corner of my eye, I see Miranda twirl the stem of her wine glass between her fingers. I can't look at Joy, either.

"In Quinta, Alice and I got to know each other a lot better. We hadn't seen each other since before I left for the US, and, well, what I'm trying to say is that we"—she pauses to quickly look at me—"we've fallen in love, Mum. Alice and I are in love."

Miranda straightens in her chair and she looks at Joy, then at me, then back to Joy, an incredulous smile splitting her face. "Excuse me, darling. Can you repeat that, please? You and Alice have fallen in love?" Her tone is high-pitched, her voice shaky. "In love?" she repeats, then starts chuckling.

Her chuckle turns into a loud cackle and then into a full-blown bout of uncontrollable laughter. Joy and I are too tense to look at each other—and I'm too perplexed by Miranda's reaction to move a muscle. I guess it's easy enough to laugh it off as a silly, grotesque joke.

"I'm all for a good joke, darling, but this is just too far out to appreciate," Miranda says when the laughter has died down.

"Mum, it's not a joke. I realise it must be hard to take in, to even understand, but this is for real. We've been seeing each other for a few weeks now." Joy tries to convince her.

"What do you mean you've been seeing each other?" For the first time since this conversation has started, Miranda looks at me. Her gaze is hard and unflinching. "What does she mean, Alice?" Her direct address makes my stomach do a flip-flop, but she doesn't give me time to reply, because she refocuses her attention on her daughter. "You see, darling, the reason why this must be a joke is because this is *Alice* you're talking about. Alice hasn't shown any romantic interest in anyone in fifteen years, and—just a little detail—if she were a lesbian, I, as her best friend, would surely know, don't you think?" Anger rises in Miranda's voice. I take it as my turn to say something.

"Miranda." There's a hitch in my voice and the middle part of her name comes out as an exasperated huff. "Though everything you just said about me used to be true, it's no longer valid."

"Oh, so seeing my daughter again has suddenly turned you gay, has it? You're a big old lesbian now. Look, I see what this is. It's menopause. I've been there, Alice, and it can be brutal. Suddenly, you find yourself questioning your very sanity. And you"—she turns to Joy again—"you've only ever displayed a very questionable taste in women. This is taking it a bit too far, granted, but, I can see that, too. I can understand how this has come about. How you've both fooled yourself into believing this is actually something to bother me with." She holds up her hands. "Well, here's my suggestion. I'm going to pretend that this conversation never happened. As soon as I walk out of this door, it will be erased from my memory. And then I will wait… I presume a few weeks, but if it takes two or three months to get this madness out of your system, then I'll just display more patience. Because I have time. I will wait until this passes and, meanwhile, you will not refer to it, neither to this evening nor this conversation. This might be real in your… hormone-crippled brains, but it certainly is not real in my life. There. That's all I have to say."

"Mum, come on." I see a tear slip down Joy's cheek. "I know this—"

"Joy, darling." Miranda's voice is unwavering. "Just stop. I'm leaving. And I'm not leaving this house with images of my daughter and my best friend"—she curls her fingers into air quotes—"'falling in love' in Portugal in my head. Do you understand me?"

"No," Joy shouts. "I will not have you do this, Mum."

I put a hand on Joy's arm to calm her down and Miranda's gaze fastens on it. She shoves her chair back and gets up. "And I will not listen to one more second of this utter nonsense."

"Let's all calm down," I offer, but I see Joy is seething with held-back rage, and Miranda clearly doesn't have a full grasp on what is happening, on how a cosy Friday evening turned into this travesty. I understand them both.

"I'm leaving, and I stand by my words." Miranda takes a pace in Joy's direction and puts a hand on her shoulder before kissing her on the top of the head. "Come by the house this weekend, darling. I have clean laundry for you." She stands still for a moment to look Joy over, then sighs. When she turns to me, she says, "Thank you for dinner, Alice." Her face is as blank as I've ever seen it. Miranda is always full of chatter, her features always brimming with emotions. This has hit her hard, and she has chosen denial to use as a coping mechanism. If I were in her shoes, I'd probably do the same.

"Fucking laundry," Joy hisses after Miranda has left. "That's what she says to me?"

"If this was the right thing to do, it sure as hell didn't feel like it," I say, ignoring Joy's rage—and probably not making it any better with my words. I just stand there, grasping the back of a chair with my hands until my knuckles go white. I can't even imagine kissing Joy after facing Miranda like this, let alone taking her to bed. It's as though confronting Miranda has made me realise—really see —who Joy is exactly. A girl I met when she was a four-hours-old baby. A baby born after her mother and I had forged our own bond. Miranda, who believed in me and took me under her wing. Miranda, whom, I believe, I have never let down as long as I have known her. And look at me now. What must she think of me now?

"Alice." Out of nowhere, Joy is by my side. "Don't let what she said get into your head. Don't forget why we told her in the first place." She touches two fingers to my arm, and I find myself shrinking away—that's how disgusted I am with myself. Because, I think, what if she's right? What if Miranda's words were the exact truth of why Joy and I are together? She's an intelligent woman, who knows much more about relationships than I do. Maybe I did just want a bright young thing to stave off a looming midlife crisis. And Miranda is doing me a huge courtesy by offering to pretend my mistake never happened.

"I'm sorry, Joy." I back away from her, only a fraction but enough to let her know that I can't bear to be touched right now. "I think I need some space to process this."

"No way, Alice." Joy pulls back a chair and sits. "If I leave now I know exactly what's going to happen. You'll get yourself into a state, you'll start panicking again, and fear will take over, and you'll make a decision you'll regret." She lets her face fall into her hands, then looks back up. "I also need you, Alice. I need you by my side. I'm not going anywhere."

I glance at beautiful, stubborn, enraged Joy and images of her life blink on and off in my mind. These images might be based on pictures Miranda has shown me over the years, or on times I actually saw Joy, I don't know. But I see her in her first school uniform. I see her doing her homework at Miranda's desk when she was seven. I see her sitting at the dinner table as a sullen teenager. I see many things, but what I don't see is a woman who is my lover. Yet, I love her. And I can't help but wonder exactly where down the line I lost myself so much that I couldn't see what was happening? When I was gripped by a madness so foreign to me it turned me into its slave. But this is life, not some fairy tale. Miranda isn't an evil witch whose plans we must thwart. She's Joy's mother. The person who loves her most in the world.

"We were wrong to do this, Joy." I want to crouch down next to her, kneel by her side, and tell her everything will be all right, but it would be as great a lie as the ones I've been feeding myself since that first kiss in Portugal. I should have stopped it there and then. Or at least should have had the wherewithal not to get involved with her in London, to have let it fade into a brooding memory—because that's all it was meant to be. "So wrong."

"Alice, I beg of you, don't do this. Not now." Joy has buried her face in her hands again. "Don't be a coward now."

"It's not cowardice. It's realism."

Joy shoots up from her chair. "I don't need this now, so fuck you, Alice. Take the weekend. Take however fucking long you want. Call me when you want to… to feel alive again." Tears stream down her cheeks. "This is bloody unbelievable."

Instead of saying her name, or taking the slightest action to keep her from leaving, I just stand there. Immobile and inert. I stand there like the coward she says I am.

After I hear my front door lock with a loud, offended bang for the second time that evening, I start to cry. I cry the way I've only cried twice in my life: when Alan left me for someone so much younger, better, and more capable as a wife; and when Paul passed away and my best friend, and her fifteen-year-old daughter were so grief-stricken I couldn't bear the unfairness of it all.

CHAPTER NINETEEN

Saturday is dreary and wretched and, in an action so unlike me I find myself staring at the ceiling instead of slipping into a restorative, forgetful sleep, I take to my bed in the middle of the afternoon. Normally, I would go to the office, but I've managed to taint the safest haven I have in this world with my foolish actions as well. Although there is no chance of Miranda being there on a Saturday afternoon—she stopped working weekends when she turned forty-five—I fear I might see her there nonetheless, that her words would linger and be amplified in the corridors of the building where we've built our professional life together.

So, instead, I swing my legs out of bed, contemplate calling Joy for the millionth time since she left last night, but decide I need some more time—just a little—and take a shower. Then, I walk. I don't care that it's raining. If anything, it's penance for the ghastly acts I've engaged in. And then, to punish me even more, a whole other set of images are projected into my mind. Joy topless. Joy pushing herself out of the pool. Joy leaning in to kiss me. Joy's hair tickling my belly while her face is buried between my legs. And then, to make matters even worse, images of me. Of me and Joy smiling, of just me grinning like an idiot. Of me smiling the sort of smile I'm not even sure I ever managed before Joy's arrival in Portugal. Of me being not-me.

Because I have no idea who I am anymore. Am I hard-working, responsible, decent Alice? Or am I lustful… joyful Alice? Or am I both? The pair of them don't seem to go together very well. And then I think of the question Joy asked me the weekend before: *is it a choice between me and my mother now?* That was not the right question to ask, however. The right question, the one that's been on my mind ever since I realised I had fallen for Joy is: *when will I be ready to choose me? Will I ever be capable?*

I walk along the streets of London, of this city that is such a part of me, and think of the other thing Joy said: *short of running away together, telling Miranda is the only option if we want to be happy.* Then my mind stops short at thoughts of Joy again. At the incredibly bright ray of sunshine she has shone into my life. How, from the dark recesses of my subconscious, she has unearthed a woman with true, valid desires, a woman who wants more from life than what she allowed herself. It's as though Joy has transported some of the Portugal sun with her, as though she soaked so much of it up when she was a child, that she travels with it wherever she goes.

My stomach starts growling because I haven't eaten anything apart from a few bites of chicken last night, so I go into a pub near Covent Garden. I thank a man who is friendly enough to hold the door open for me and I stare straight into a face I would recognise anywhere, anytime, no matter the amount of wrinkles that have accumulated, and the vast distance his hairline has receded: the face of my ex-husband.

"Alice," he says.

"Christ," I mutter, "Alan." As though saying each other's name will make this less awkward.

"It's been a while." he says.

Quite the understatement, I think. "It has. How have you been?" I couldn't be less interested in the physical—let alone emotional—well-being of the man who left me, but it's that pesky ingrained politeness that just won't leave me be.

"Good. And you? My goodness, it really has been ages." We stand there, with the door still half-open, until he lets the knob slip from his hand and it falls shut behind me. "I was just leaving, but I have time for a drink. What do you say?"

Say no, I tell myself. By all means, say no. "Of course," I say, because with Alan, the old Alice thrived. We never had children, but another person was birthed while we were married: this version of me that I'm now so desperately trying to cling on to. The one who's so adamant to push Joy away.

"Splendid. Why don't you sit down and I'll get us a drink. Earl Grey tea?" he asks, presumptuously.

"I'll have a glass of red wine, please." I take a good look at his face while I make my request. Despite the extra wrinkles and the hair loss, he looks good for a man of his age. His posture is straight-backed, and there's no sign of a paunch beneath his sports jacket. Yet, the mere thought of waking up with a man like him—the way I would have done if we hadn't divorced—chills me to my core.

Alan regards me with those heavy-lidded eyes of his, as if to say: are you sure you want to drink an alcoholic beverage at this time of the day. "Coming right up."

When he returns and deposits our drinks on the table, I'm mostly baffled by how much I don't care about learning anything about his life. Not because it's too painful—on the contrary. Time has done its bit. My wounds have healed and all the scar tissue has, in fact, disintegrated. He's just a man sitting across from me. And, if he's anything to me, he's a glimpse into the future I could have had. We could be sitting in this pub as husband and wife. A completely legitimate couple of whom no one would ask themselves any questions. Not like when I'm out with Joy and I'm always a little ill at ease. But at what cost does it come? I wonder. What price am I willing to pay to appear conventional, to avoid upsetting complete strangers, people who know absolutely nothing about my life?

"Still going strong at Jones & McAllister?" he asks.

"Business is thriving." As I say the words, I can't help but wonder what I'm doing sitting in this touristy pub with my ex-husband, a man who sparks zero emotions within me, when I could be spending the weekend with a woman whom I love. A woman who, compared to this man that I married and intended to spend the rest of my life with, has given me ten times more pleasure in a few weeks than he did in years. "Alan, I'm very sorry. Thank you for the wine, but I just realised I have to be somewhere. It slipped my mind. It was good seeing you. I hope you and Sheryl are well." I push myself out of the booth and hold out my hand.

Perplexed, he takes it in his and gives it a limp shake.

"Goodbye," I say and hurry out of the pub, already stretching out my arm to hail a cab. Alan was not a bad man. Our marriage was conventional, proper, something both our parents and all of our friends and colleagues could approve of. It was passionate for about five minutes. And for the longest time, I believed it was all I wanted in life. When I lost it, I was shattered by the loss of something I was taught to desire. But the main reason why I never had much interest in investing myself fully in another affair with a man my age— someone deemed appropriate for me—is because I, honestly, couldn't be bothered. If that was it, then what was the point? I never wanted another Alan. And other Alans were all I saw, until Joy got out of that yellow Mini in the Algarve and made my world spin on its axis.

Besides, if my husband can leave me for a younger woman, why can't I, a free, single woman, be with one? But this is hardly a feminist, or even a fairness issue. Not because I know that life isn't always fair, but because it's so much more than that. It's the new zest for life I've felt coursing through my veins. It's watching Joy sleep peacefully on her back, obliviously, and thinking: *I will always be here for you. I will never hurt you. I want you to reach the maximum potential of happiness in your life. I love you. I want you.*

A cab finally stops and I direct the driver to Joy's street

in Shoreditch. Because I know it's not a choice, but if it were, I *would* choose her. God, I hope she's home. Traffic is slow, as usual. Should I call her? Maybe she's picking up her laundry at Miranda's. Why does she not own a washing machine at the brink of thirty? My mind races, and I feel frazzled, dizzy almost, but also deliriously happy and stupidly optimistic. Because, perhaps for the first time in my life—and, ironically, I have my ex-husband to thank for this realisation—I don't care what anyone thinks of me, or expects from me. I choose love and passion. I choose Joy, and I choose me.

★ ★ ★

"That took you long enough," Joy says when I reach her flat. I got out of the cab a few streets from her building, so fed up with the pace of traffic, that I decided to walk. And I didn't care what anyone thought of that middle-aged woman hurrying down the street, her cheeks flushed and the sides of her trench coat flapping behind her in the wind. Because that woman was on her way to tell the person she loves once and for all that, yes, she *was* right. Telling Miranda was the only possible solution.

I need to catch my breath after climbing the stairs and while I do, I notice a bag of ironed blouses and t-shirts on the kitchen table. "You went to see Miranda?"

"I did," Joy says. "Jeff was back and he clearly didn't know, so either she hadn't had the chance to tell him, or she's really sticking to her foolish plan of denial. She did fold my laundry, though."

"I'm sorry for freaking out last night, Joy. I can assure you, with my hand on my heart, it will never happen again."

"Good." She cocks her head to the right. "I'm glad you came. I was about to go on a bender."

"Oh really?" I could be snarky, and ask if that's her solution to everything, but if this is a comparison of flaws, or even of destructive behaviour, I'm sure I would come out on top.

"Yes, but now I have a different kind of bender in mind."

"Don't keep me in suspense." I walk over to Joy, as if pulled towards her by an invisible rope—and hasn't it felt like that from the very beginning?

"You're very much a part of it." She puts her arms on my shoulders and stares into my eyes. "You, naked, in the sheets that Mum washed." Her giggle is infectious and I snicker with her, because, really, what else are we going to do?

When we're done laughing, I tell her in all earnestness, "You can do your laundry at my house from now on."

CHAPTER TWENTY

At work the next Monday, Miranda is her usual chatty self. I don't want to provoke her by saying something untoward, but in many ways, this stand-off, this charade, is much worse than being with Joy behind her back. I also realise Miranda will need time, and lots of it, to come to terms with our relationship. I'm not expecting family dinners any time soon. But love is the most powerful motivator of human action in this world. Miranda loves Joy. I love Joy. We have to discuss this.

"Can we talk?" I knock on her door just before lunch.

"If it's about work, I'm all ears." She doesn't look up from her computer.

I don't confirm this intention, nor wait for an invitation to continue. Instead, I close the door and sit. "It's not about work."

Miranda plants her fingertips on the tabletop and inhales deeply twice, before looking at me. "Alice, if you've come in here to further ruin our friendship, then please be my guest, but don't expect anything from me. Not a response, and especially not some words of acceptance. Joy is my child and I simply won't have it."

"I haven't come to seek acceptance, Miranda. And yes, Joy is your daughter, but she's not a child anymore. She hasn't been for a long time. She's suffering because of this. I understand denial as a first line of defence very well, but you ignoring this… important thing in her life is hurting her."

"*She's* hurting. *She's* suffering. That's a good one." Miranda's spine is rigid as a broomstick, her voice icy and unemotional. "What did you think, Alice? That a weekend of rest and relaxation would solve the issue for me in my head? That I would step into the office today a different woman? That I wouldn't care anymore who Joy is *seeing*? It's not because I refuse to accept, even for a single second, that this is happening, that it doesn't hurt me. In fact, it makes me sick to my stomach. And I will deal with my daughter in the way that I see fit. I don't need your advice, thank you very much." At last, she relaxes her muscles and leans against the backrest of her chair. "By the way, now that we are freely dispensing advice… I know my daughter much better than you do. And, well, she will grow tired of you sooner rather than later. That's not even wishful thinking on my part. It's a given. I love her dearly, but she seems incapable of staying with the same person longer than a few months. That's not going to change for the mighty Alice McAllister, you know? Best brace yourself for some heartache."

"I understand you're saying this because you're upset —"

Miranda cuts me off. "You're completely delusional, Alice. You leave for Portugal an over-worked, straight woman and you come back a lesbian who's in love with my daughter… Have you even stopped to think how ludicrous that is? I know the sun can be rather strong down south, and something must have really gone wrong for you to believe all these, frankly, insane words that keep on coming from your mouth."

"Okay." I rise. "It was a mistake to come in here."

"Not the only mistake you've made lately," Miranda hurls at me as I exit her office. In the hallway, I steel myself, not willing to let anyone see how shaken I am. I lock myself in my own office, forego lunch, and think of ways to win over my friend. I come up empty.

★ ★ ★

In the evening, when I meet Joy for dinner, I give her the broad strokes of what Miranda said, leaving out the comments about Joy's flakiness in relationships.

"I want to instate a rule," Joy says, in reply. "Obviously, Mum is a very important person in both our lives, but we can't let her take over our relationship. So here is my suggestion: we say what we have to say about her in the first five to ten minutes we're together, then we move on. We're all waiting here. She's waiting for it to pass, while we're waiting for her to come to terms with the fact that it won't. We can spend our time deconstructing every little thing she says, but it's not going to do us much good, is it? All we can do is wait and give her time. We can't expect miracles."

"You're wise beyond your years," I say, no longer feeling the hunger I came to the table with because I want her so much.

"I know. My wisdom is wasted on people my own age. That's why I hang with the likes of you." She gives me one of those smiles that make me melt. And melt I do, but not without wondering if we *can* actually do this. If we can wait Miranda out without causing too much damage.

"So we wait," I say. "Whatever shall we do with ourselves while we do?"

"I can think of a thing or two." Joy is in full seduction mode—not that she needs to be. "There's Bobby's photo exhibition next week. And I really want to go see that play that's on at the Young Vic. And my new colleague, Clare, has invited us to Juno's baby shower."

"Juno?" All these plans I didn't use to have, I think while I ask Joy. "What kind of a name is that?"

"It's modern." Joy just shrugs. "And, did it fail to register that I said she invited *us*? I've started telling people at work about my significant other. It's such a thrill, Alice. These are people I only met after we got together and it feels so good to just be able to blurt things out about us without getting any quizzical looks because they know who you are."

"Unlike your friends who came to your house the other day and had to smoke a joint to deal with the pressure of not mentioning Miranda."

"They were doing their best. Bless them. But I won't make that mistake again"

"This is an unusual situation to be in, but one I wouldn't want to miss." I reach for her hand on the table in a gesture of what Joy taught me a few days ago is called PDA. "But the very last thing I want is for you to fall out with your mother over me. She's stubborn, like you."

Joy is so at ease with herself she takes my hand in hers without so much as blinking. "Did I like it when she started seeing Jeff, when I walked in on them groping each other in the kitchen, and when she moved him into our house? I most certainly did not. But did I learn to live with it? Oh yes, I did. Because that's just what we do for family. I wanted Mum to be happy again after Dad died. That's why I'm saying we should wait her out. It took a long time for me to accept Jeff. But I did, in the end. That's how I know Mum will come around. She has no choice and, most importantly, she wants me to be happy." She squeezes my hand. "You make me happy, Alice. Happier than I've been before. She'll take notice."

Miranda's words from earlier today flit through my head again. Joy must have noticed because when I don't immediately reply, she asks, "What is it?"

"Nothing." I'm torn between giving into my own insecurities and telling her what Miranda said about Joy's propensity for short affairs, and protecting Joy by never having her find out what Miranda said about her in the heat of the moment.

"Tell me, Alice, please. Let's not have secrets, no matter how small."

"Okay." I take a deep breath. "When I spoke to Miranda today she told me I was delusional to think that you would stay with me. That I had better prepare myself for a bout of heartbreak because you don't really do long-term relationships."

Joy sighs. "What would she know about that, really? I mean, sadly enough, I can understand why she would say such a thing, especially under the current circumstances and to you, but it couldn't be less true." She looks at our intertwined fingers for an instant. "She has only just come to terms with me being a lesbian. I wasn't going to tell her about why my relationship with Tamsin failed. And, granted, Alex was a mistake. That was never meant to last. But I'm only twenty-nine. What does she want? For me to have a proven track record of monogamy before I'm thirty? She was just lashing out, Alice, because she doesn't even want to consider how much I care for you." She gazes into my eyes. "I can only hope you didn't believe her."

"Not for a second." Whether it's the truth, or a half-truth, doesn't even matter in this moment. When Joy looks at me like this, there isn't a shadow of a doubt in my mind that she has anything but good intentions for our relationship.

"But now we're talking about Mum again." Her lips curve into a lopsided smile.

"I know. I don't have many friends like Miranda. In fact, I have none."

"Speaking of friends. I have every intention of showing you off to every person I know in the coming months. Is there anyone you want to introduce me to? I'll be good, I promise."

Is there? I hadn't even given it a second thought. My life consists of work, the occasional work-related social gathering, dinner once in a while at Miranda's, and going to the opera or a museum maybe once or twice a month. I feel suddenly embarrassed by this. Not because it displays a huge lack of social prowess, but because it makes me realise exactly how much of my time I single-mindedly devote to my job. "I'm not sure. My parents are no longer with us. My sister lives in Budapest and I see her once a year if I'm lucky —or unlucky, depending on how you look upon it. I'm afraid I really do spend most of my time if not working, then at least thinking about it."

"God, Alice. I can see why Mum wanted you as a business partner. That woman is one smart cookie. You must regret the 50/50 split equity because you have made her rich. Your hard work has basically funded my college education. And that house in Portugal is as much yours as it is hers."

"Miranda had a family. It was different for her. I've never begrudged her anything because if it hadn't been for her I might still be working for someone else. She pushed me to take the risk, and the risk paid off."

"Risk? It's not a risk when you work eighty hours per week, Alice. My mother is conniving enough to have seen that in you." She regards me with a pensive look. "And you had a family when you started out. You had Alan. Did you never want to have children?"

I shake my head. "When I look back now, I have to say no. But back in the day, after you were married, it was just automatically assumed that the woman would get pregnant, but I never did. I could have pursued it more. I would have if I really wanted to. But I guess I didn't."

"What do you mean? You couldn't have children? Or your ex couldn't?"

"Well, Alan certainly can. He has a child with Sheryl." There was a time when saying this would have somehow made me feel mortified—not sad, but inadequate, I guess. "Technically, I can have children. I've had everything thoroughly examined. It's just not as straightforward as with most people. It would have involved a lot of tracking, charts and intercourse I didn't really feel like having." Then, I'm hit with the first inkling of a thought I most definitely don't want to have. I can choose: push it away and ignore it, or just ask Joy. The longer I let the thought linger in my brain, the less of a choice I seem to have. I have to ask her this, and I have to ask her now. "How about you? Do you want children?" There's a good reason why asking Joy this hadn't crossed my mind yet. I'm fifty-one and never had a pronounced child wish, and the past two months, my mind has been so occupied with new emotion after new emotion. But Joy is so young, and I'm so terrified by her upcoming response I break out in a cold sweat.

"I don't know." Her gaze is no longer pinned on me, instead it drifts into the distance. "I've never been in a situation where I really had to ask myself that question. I never had to see a doctor to have the pill prescribed, for instance. I never had to worry about a condom breaking or the morning-after pill. And I've never been in a relationship where the question might have popped up."

"Yes, but aside from circumstance." I tap my chest with my free hand. "In here. How do you feel about it?"

"I really don't know, Alice. I'm not the kind of person who is preoccupied with faraway notions like that. But if you're asking whether I can feel my clock ticking and whether I have a growing, burning desire to be *with child*, I haven't. This may change. I don't know."

Another something Miranda can resent me for, I think. Taking away her chance at a grandchild. "It really is too early for this conversation." There's a nervous tremor in my voice.

"I don't think it is," Joy is quick to say. "As long as we're open with each other about what we want." She looks at me again. "Look, Alice, I know that my, uh, cougar love"—she inserts a chuckle—"comes with certain consequences. But I wouldn't worry about me asking you to become a mother in five years' time. I know what I'm getting myself into here. I'm not naive."

The answer to this particular question was never going to be wholly satisfying, but for now, in these early stages of our affair, I can still easily push the worry to the back of my mind. After all, not every woman is destined to be a mother —and thank goodness for that.

CHAPTER TWENTY-ONE

Time moves on and three and a half weeks go by during which I immerse myself into work even more with the dual intention of freeing up my spare time for Joy and being so busy I barely have time to notice Miranda. When we find ourselves in a room together, we perform our charade. And Miranda can pretend that what she doesn't want to happen isn't happening, but it is, and I can see the effects of her denial so plainly on her face, it makes me wonder what our co-workers think of her appearance. Joy has been keeping her distance from her mother as well, and that must hurt her even more.

But I stick to the plan, and I wait. Which is, in the end, easier than another confrontation. Although I know that in the long run the situation is untenable, for now, it's just how things are. Until one afternoon, Miranda cracks, and barges into my office without a knock—something she's never done, no matter how long we've worked together—and sits without invitation.

"I need to say something," she announces.

I brace myself for an outburst of rage, or at least for a bout of passive-aggressive reasoning. "Of course," I say.

"I want to retire." Her words are measured, her vowels clipped. "I'm turning fifty-nine next month. I've had enough. I've worked enough."

Of all the things I had expected Miranda to throw at me, this one really comes out of left field. Miranda has certainly scaled back her workload, but there has never been any mention of stopping work. Besides, fifty-nine is not a proper retirement age. She has at least ten more good work years ahead of her. "Really?" I figure it's best to let her talk.

"Yes," is all she says, which confirms my suspicion that this is about Joy and me and not so much about her wanting to retire.

"If this is what you really want, we should of course discuss it, but are you sure? This is a big step. You are a founding partner of this firm."

"I'm sure you can handle it alone, Alice."

"This just seems to come out of the blue. You've never mentioned it before."

"Well, that's probably because I lost my best friend. But don't you dare blame me for not confiding in you anymore. And if you really want to know: I can't work with you anymore. I can't stand the sight of your smug face walking in here every morning. I barely see my daughter anymore, because of course, now, this is all my fault. So, yes, I've lost my best friend and my daughter, and I'm willing to throw in my half of the company as well. How's that for sacrifice?"

"I am very sorry you feel that way." A lump lodges itself at the back of my throat.

"Joy may very well be the happiest she's ever been, but I don't know, because half the time she refuses to pick up when I call. She doesn't come around anymore, not even to do her laundry. Are you doing her laundry now, Alice? Are you her girlfriend"—she can't possibly make the word sound any more vile—"*and* her mother now?"

"You know why she's keeping her distance. If only you could give in a tiny bit—"

"A tiny bit? And then what? More and more until I actually accept this farce?" She shakes her head vigorously. "You can dream all you want, Alice. It's never going to happen. I will never accept you and Joy being together and I certainly will never give you my blessing."

Are you really willing to lose your daughter over this? I want to ask, but it's not a fair question. Moreover, I can see

Miranda's pure agony. And it's not as though she made her own bed of misery all by herself. This is my fault. I am responsible for this.

"Have you spoken to anyone about this at all? Or are you bottling it all up?"

"The only one who knows is Jeff. But I certainly haven't gone around shouting it from the rooftops. The whole thing is way too sordid for that."

"I'm sorry you still feel that way." Apologies are all I have.

Miranda bows her head to rub her temples, then looks back up at me. "How is she? How is my girl doing?" And I can hear the pain in her voice, the sheer agony of having to ask *me*, of all people, this question.

I weigh my response, but Miranda has always been brutally honest with me as far as this subject is concerned, so I may as well be the same with her. "She's happy and unhappy at the same time, because how can she be truly happy when her mother rejects her?"

"I don't reject *her*." Miranda sounds close to sobbing. "I don't even reject her lifestyle… I just… can't… I can't even properly say it. And maybe that's stubborn, or foolish even, but I just can't, Alice. And it's not a reflection on you as a person, although I will never see you in the same light again, it's the simple thought of you and her together. You're like a sister to me. You have seen her grow up. And she's so young. I—I…" She shakes her head again. "I've tried to open my mind, and to think of Joy as happy with you, but it just doesn't compute in my brain. The number of times I've heard Joy repeat those words in my head: Alice and I have fallen in love. That's exactly the number of times I have found myself repulsed by the mere notion.

"And now I'm sitting here, greatly offending you. *You*, Alice, my best friend. Because this should not be happening. It's not right. It will never be, no matter how long you give me. Just try… try to put yourself in my position. I know you don't have children and it might be hard for you to imagine, but just try to walk in my shoes, if only for an hour, and you *will* understand. You will understand why I can't be any other way about this."

She's right. I *am* offended. Flabbergasted, in fact, that Miranda would speak to me like that, like I'm some dirty old man who has snatched her daughter away from her, who has soiled Joy, perverted her, while what Joy and I have is exactly the opposite.

"And resigning will make that better?" I ask, because I refuse to defend myself any more. I have put myself in Miranda's position every single day since Joy and I got together, and I feel her pain, and I understand her scepticism, even her anger. But the only way I can make her life better is by ending my relationship with Joy. And I decided weeks ago not to do that. But I can't sit here and explain to her how her daughter has revived me, how much she has changed me and my life. That would only make matters worse, I'm sure.

"It's not the most ideal solution, of course, but at least I won't have to see you any more."

While I've put up with all the things Miranda has said to me, and has insinuated about me, in a polite, respectful way up until now, this is the final straw. These words, coming from her mouth, hurt me to my very core. I call on my most icy voice when I say, "Fine. If that's how you want it."

A heavy silence hangs in the room for long, agonising minutes. "It is," Miranda finally says.

"Then please get out of my office now." Because if she doesn't, I will fall apart in front of her, and I don't want to give her the satisfaction. Miranda doesn't deserve to see me cry.

She gets up, unsteadily. "Look, Alice…" I detect the slightest hint of regret in her voice. "Some things are said —"

"Just get out, Miranda. Just leave me be." My voice is

crumbling already. "Just go."

She casts me one last glance, and I can't tell if it's a contemptuous one, or a pitiful one, or one filled with rage, because I avert my eyes when she looks at me. I'm guilty, too. I'm most guilty of all.

I only look up when I hear the door slam shut, and I'm grateful it's closed because the tears come again. I used to be one of those women who hardly ever cried because I had become so used to bottling it all up, to let the tears dry up before they had a chance to roll from my eyes.

"God damn you, Alice," I say to myself. "God damn you." Because this is not a love without grave repercussions, and Joy's waiting-game plan seems to be failing miserably.

✶ ✶ ✶

I hadn't planned on seeing Joy that evening, but I'm so upset I ask her to cancel her plans with Marcy and come to my house.

"It's not working," I say to Joy in a level voice, because I've cried my tears by then, and I've expelled the rage from my voice. "Your mother isn't going to budge." I tell her about how Miranda all but called me a pervert, and about how she wants to retire from the firm so she doesn't have to look at my smug face anymore.

"Jesus, Alice. She's really losing it," Joy replies. "She has really gone and lost her mind."

"We have done this to her," I say.

Joy ignores my comment. "The woman you have just described is not my mother. That is not the same person who raised me, who told me every day I was the most precious thing in her life, and who hugs me so tightly sometimes, I have to peel her off me. I don't know what, but we're going to have to do something. Maybe talk to Jeff."

"It's not you she has the issue with, Joy. It's me. She misses you so much. She told me so."

"Maybe I should talk to her. However badly Mum is feeling, perhaps this is the moment we've been waiting for, and it can go either way now." Joy's tone brightens. "I should go to her now. She's cracking. Maybe she'll be open to, at the very least, talk about it with me, which would be huge progress."

"I don't know. Maybe you should let her cool off some more. If you go over now she might feel as though I sent you—and she will certainly get the impression we've been talking about her."

"Of course, we talk about her. Everything she has said since we told her warrants a long discussion."

"Good grief, Joy. Is there a manual somewhere about this that we can consult? Can we Google the solution to this problem?"

This brings a tiny smile to Joy's face. "Fuck it, Alice. I'm going over. I'm going to talk some sense into my mother."

If only it were that easy, I think. "Good luck with that."

"I'll be back." She kisses me hard on the lips before heading out the door.

All I can do is wait. And ponder, once again, if it's all worth it. I reprimand myself instantly for even thinking that, because I know, above all else, that it is.

★ ★ ★

Joy returns not even an hour later.

"Mum was asleep. Apparently she took a sleeping pill. So I had to deal with Jeff," she says laconically. "He was quite a good sport about it, actually."

"What did he say?" I slide to the edge of my seat.

"Well, he did start by stating he thinks she's close to a nervous breakdown. Because she feels so torn. She has told him that the last thing she wants is to push me away, but the second-last thing she wants is me in a relationship with you."

I sigh, because it feels as though it's going to be like this for the rest of time. "Does Jeff have an opinion on all of this?"

Joy quirks up her eyebrows. "When does Jeff *not* have

an opinion?""

"True enough." If we can't mock Jeff a little now, just to make ourselves feel better, when can we?

"But, he was very non-Jeff-y about it, actually. He said things like, 'I understand you can't sacrifice love to make your mother happy'. Can you imagine these words coming from his mouth? It was a bit surreal."

"People can surprise you when you least expect it."

"He's going to tell Mum I stopped by and I promised to pick up when she calls me."

"How are you feeling?" I ask, shuffling to the side of the sofa and gesturing for Joy to come sit.

"Exhausted," Joy says as she crashes down next to me. She puts her head on my shoulder. "This is not how it's supposed to be, Alice. We're in the honeymoon stage of our relationship. We should be having sex on this very sofa right now instead of worrying about what Mum thinks of us."

"Mmm," I murmur. She's right. After the things Miranda said to me today, and after hearing her mentioned in a sentence referring to our sex life, the last thing I want to do is push Joy down and kiss her until the morning light.

CHAPTER TWENTY-TWO

As days bleed into weeks, it becomes increasingly more difficult to adhere to my split personality of trying to block out all emotions at work, and being my new passionate self after hours. Miranda hasn't said anything significant to me, nor has she elaborated on her plan to retire. Until one day, from the open door of my office, I see her leave the building for the night without so much as saying goodbye to me again —hellos and goodbyes have become a rarity; we only exchange niceties in front of clients now—and I realise I miss her. Being in the same building with her from Monday to Friday makes it much worse. I wish she'd already retired. I fully understand the sentiment now. If this is how things are going to be between us, it *is* just too hard.

"Something's going to have to give at some point," I say to Joy on a Friday evening after a day during which I've barely seen Miranda. The few times I did, it felt as though her initial rage had transformed into a deep, unspeakable sadness. In the break room that afternoon, when I walked in to fetch a cup of tea, she stood there gazing in front of her, leaning against the fridge with her hip, and I didn't meet the usual condescension in her stare, only resignation—as though she was coming to terms with the inevitable. She didn't say anything, though, just straightened her spine and walked right past me.

"I miss her so much. She's my mum," Joy replies. The conversations we have seem to repeat themselves on a daily basis. "We used to speak at least every other day. Even when I was in the US." I remember the astronomical phone bills—

of which I never said anything to Miranda—at Jones & McAllister well enough. "And now, even when we do speak, it's just not the same. We dance around the subject, like we're walking on a tightrope. And I can sense that she's trying, but every time the subject could possibly drift towards you, there's this silence. This unbreakable wall."

"I know." We're at Joy's flat, getting ready to go out— even though I'm tired and I'd much rather stay in after the draining week I've had at work. I, too, miss Miranda so much. I miss her energy around me. The way we used to discuss every tiny detail of our business, not because it was necessary, but because we enjoyed doing it. Because it made us feel proud and accomplished. "It's ridiculous how, every time I check our joint calendar, I'm relieved to find she'll be out of the office for a few hours." Earlier this week I noticed Miranda had a gynaecologist appointment scheduled for this morning—being angry with me hasn't curbed her over-sharing tendencies. Although she has been adding less personal appointments to the calendar, and it could be that this particular doctor's visit has been scheduled for months.

"Okay." Joy turns to me. "We've reached our limit for today." She taps her fingers against the palm of her hand. "Time out starts now."

"Deal," I say, looking at myself in the mirror. "Tell me why exactly we have to go to this exhibition again after we've already attended the opening three weeks ago?"

"Because Bobby is my friend—*our* friend—and we want to support him on his closing night."

"I'm too old for this, you know?" I chuckle, because I know what's coming next.

"Nu-uh, you don't get to play the age card." Joy walks towards me and pushes me against the wall. "Because if you're too old to go out with me to a very upstanding, civilised, early activity, you are surely also too old for this." She nuzzles my neck. "And this." She sinks her teeth into my earlobe. "And for what I bought for you."

That's a new one. "What did you buy?"

"You'll see. Tomorrow. If you're good." Her body is still pressed against mine, her hot breath on my face.

"If I'm good? I'm *always* good." I curl my arms around her neck and gaze into her eyes. Every time I look into her eyes like that, I'm reminded of the astounding transformation I have gone through by falling in love with her.

"I'll be the judge of that," Joy says, before kissing me, and smearing my lips with her freshly-applied lipstick.

★ ★ ★

At the gallery, I mainly talk to Justin. Joy teased me and said I like him so much because he's closest to me in age, but he's just a very easy person to talk to, despite the number of expletives that leave his mouth a mile a minute.

We're chit-chatting next to, according to what I've been told, a picture of Justin, although you can't see Justin's face in it, and the contorted shape his body is portrayed in isn't recognisable to me at all.

"This one isn't for sale. Only for artistic merit," Justin says, as he gazes at it. "Bobby wanted my face on it, but I managed to convince him my old mug is too ugly for a beautiful picture." His gaze shifts from the picture to me. "Now, you though, Alice. I bet you photograph really well. You have this whole aristocratic thing going on. That patrician nose, those cheekbones, that naughty glint you get in your eyes sometimes. I mean, I can surely see why Joy is so crazy about you."

By now, I've got used to Justin saying things like that to me. The first time he complimented my looks, I blushed all the way up from my shoulders to my scalp. "Why thank you, young sir," I jest, feeling more flattered than embarrassed.

"I'd like to introduce you to some friends of mine, if you don't mind." He starts waving at two men who are examining the picture next to the one of him. One of them must be my age, I suspect. He's wearing a suit and his greying hair appears quite thin. The other one looks more like a teenager than a grown-up, leading me, at first, to believe that he is the older guy's son. "These are Jeremy and Tim. Jeremy is one of my oldest friends, and he just got back from jet-setting around the world, where he encountered this gem of a man."

"Nice to meet you." Jeremy offers his hand, and I shake it. "Don't believe a word this one says, by the way. I was working very hard in Singapore for five years, where I did, indeed, meet Tim."

"Hi." Tim is less formal in his greeting, and seems to sport one of those carefree American accents.

So this is what it feels like for perfect strangers when they meet me and Joy, I think. Because even though I might have briefly considered that Tim was Jeremy's son, that doesn't mean I didn't instinctively know they are, in fact, a couple.

"I'm Alice. Very pleased to meet you."

"Alice is Joy's partner," Justin says while he points at Joy who is standing a few feet away.

"Oh, I spoke to her earlier. What a lovely girl. You seem to have picked up some friends who are much posher than you while I was away, Jussie," Jeremy says. "Are you finally growing up?"

"Nah," Justin replies, "I just got tired of hanging with the trashy likes of you." They banter back and forth, while Tim and I become less and less involved in their old-chums conversation.

"So you moved here from Singapore?" I ask Tim, because I'm curious to find out about their situation.

"Yes. Quite the temperature difference," he says. "Is it always so cold here?" He paints the sweetest smile on his face.

"I'm afraid this is nothing compared to what's yet to come." From behind Tim, I see Joy making her way towards me, and I'm suddenly very aware of how far removed from my old life I find myself, talking to this young man I don't know at a photo exhibition in Hoxton where all the pictures are, quite frankly, extremely homo-erotic and not to my taste at all. "Winter is coming." I have to suppress a chuckle as I say the phrase, because I only picked it up after watching a horrendously bloody and violent TV show with Joy where that seems to be the phrase *de rigueur*.

"Do you watch *Game of Thrones*?" Tim asks me with a sparkle in his eyes, and I find myself wondering if he and Jeremy watch it together, and whether Jeremy thinks it's ghastly as well.

"Not if I can help it."

"Hey," Joy says when she joins us. "Hi again, Tim." Her arrival seems to snap Jeremy and Justin out of their private conversation.

"Are you all coming back to our house to celebrate Bobby's successful show?" Justin asks.

"Sure," Jeremy says, without consulting Tim, and I fervently hope Joy won't do the same and speak for us both without checking with me first. It's ten o'clock. I'm tired. And I'm not the kind of person who goes back to someone else's house this late in the day.

Justin eyes Joy expectantly.

"I need to check with my missus," she says, to my great relief. Although I can tell she wants to go, and why should she not? It's Friday evening. She should go out with her friends, have too much to drink, and laugh the night away. But going-out protocol is not something we have discussed at length, apart from my insistence that Joy do whatever comes natural to her.

"You go ahead," I say to Joy. "It's way past my bedtime." I give a brief chuckle to hide how uncomfortable this is making me feel.

She gazes at me for an instant to, I imagine, try to read my face. "That's okay. I'll take a rain check. I'm beat, too."

"Aah, these youngsters," Jeremy laments, "they don't

make them like us anymore, do they, Jus?" With that, they slip back into their energetic conversation from before, teasing each other mercilessly.

Joy stands next to me and drapes her arm over my shoulder.

"I really don't mind if you go," I say, wanting to make it perfectly clear that I'm *cool* with this.

"I know," Joy whispers in my ear, "but I'd rather spend time with you." Next, she plants a gentle kiss on my cheek— and Tim is left smiling perplexedly at us. Perhaps with exactly the same facial expression as I had when I looked at him and Jeremy earlier.

✶ ✶ ✶

On the way home, Joy's arm linked through mine, her body leaning into me as we walk, I ask, "How old do you think Tim is?"

"Hard to tell. He's Asian, so he's probably forty but looks twenty," Joy says. "Why?"

"Just wondering." I can't keep the trepidation out of my tone, though.

"Alice McAllister, don't tell me you think Jeremy is too old for him?" There's a smile in her voice.

"I don't think anything of the sort, it was just… confrontational, I guess, for me to be introduced to another couple with a visible, significant age difference between them."

"How did it make you feel?" Joy leans in a bit closer.

I try to find the right words before I speak. "Not as self-conscious as I thought it would."

"The strangest combinations of people fall in love, Alice. It's what makes the world go round. As long as it makes them happy."

"And as long as they're equals in the relationship," I add.

"What does that even mean? Equals?" Joy asks. "I stand by *my* words: as long as they're both happy."

Just as we turn the corner to Joy's street, her phone starts ringing. She sighs. "I bet that's Justin wanting to nag me about not accepting his invitation." She digs her phone out of her coat pocket and stares at the screen. "It's Mum," she says.

"This late?" I say, but Joy doesn't hear me because she's already answering Miranda's call.

"Hello, Mum?" she says. "Mum, calm down. What's going on?" Joy looks at me as though she has no idea what her mother is saying. If Miranda is that incoherent, she's either drunk, or something terrible has happened. I'm beginning to fear the latter. Joy holds the phone away from her ear for an instant and addresses me, "See if you can find us a taxi, Alice." Then she goes back to calming Miranda down on the phone. All sorts of thoughts immediately flit through my brain. Did Jeff have a heart attack? Did she take a nasty fall? Frantically, I look around for a taxi. The benefit of Joy's neighbourhood is that on a Friday evening a ton of people come and go and I manage to flag one down almost immediately.

I give the driver Miranda's address, because that's where I think we're headed, then look for confirmation on Joy's face. She nods, while listening to her mother on the phone. Joy has gone silent, which leads me to believe Miranda has quietened down.

"Okay, Mum, listen, we're on our way," Joy says. "We'll be there in fifteen minutes. I love you."

After Joy hangs up she looks at me, her face drained of all colour. "At her gynaecologist appointment today, they found a lump in her breast. Her doctor sent her for a mammogram and ultrasound, but they don't know what it is for sure and now she needs a biopsy."

CHAPTER TWENTY-THREE

Jeff opens the door for us, then steps out and closes it behind his back to speak to us in private. "She's had a bit too much. She's very upset," he says.

"I want to see her." Joy's voice is urgent. She doesn't wait for Jeff to let her in, but pushes the door open and heads into the house.

"Hi Alice," Jeff says as we shuffle inside behind Joy. I haven't seen him since that dinner party Joy trapped me into. "God, I'm glad you're here." Jeff has always had a dramatic streak, nevertheless, the words are a relief to hear.

"What do you know?" I ask.

"When I came home from work," he whispers, "she was already plastered. She was sitting on the sofa with a half-empty bottle of sherry in front of her. She told me about the lump, and the mammogram and ultrasound, and I tried to talk to her, made her some dinner, but she just kept on drinking." He coughs. "She wasn't exactly in an optimal state of mind to receive bad news, and well, I guess it brought back some very depressing memories."

Poor, poor Miranda, I think. And she didn't have her best friend to call. I vow there and then to, whether she wants me to or not, worm my way into her life again. I need her and she needs me.

When I enter the living room, Joy and Miranda are standing in a hug so tight it looks as though they can never break from it. Poor Joy, I think then. She has seen her father die from cancer, and now this. But, as far as I know—and I don't know much—it could very well be benign. This is what we must focus on.

Miranda is crying big heaving sobs on Joy's shoulder and Jeff and I just stand there, mute spectators to this mother-daughter reunion. But they need this moment together more than anything. So I wait, shuffling my weight around awkwardly, my heart in my throat. What if it's *not* benign? Miranda knows all about the long torturous road of chemo and endless doctor and hospital visits, and she also knows that, no matter how good the care—and how high the hopes—the outcome isn't always positive. Paul didn't survive.

Moreover, Joy is Paul's daughter as well, and I was the primary cause of this rift between Joy and her mother. Me, Miranda's best friend. It's so abysmal I find myself thinking in Joy-terms: this is so *fucked-up*. So bloody fucked-up. And we need to fix this right now, because Miranda needs all of us by her side. The most important thing is that she doesn't feel alone—and how alone must she have felt the past weeks? She probably felt that Joy and I were against her.

When they break from their hug, Miranda is wobbly on her legs, and I fear the instant she lays eyes on me.

"Alice," she says, her voice breaking.

I rush over to her and take her into my arms, which I haven't done since Paul's death—Miranda and I never had a hugging kind of friendship. I hold her for long moments and let it all fall away, because, in the face of this, any hurtful words that have been spoken between us have no more importance. We all have a single-minded goal now, one that doesn't involve acceptance of who's with who, or early retirement because of a crumbling friendship. Miranda, Jeff, Joy and I only want for Miranda's lump to not be life-threatening. And, if it is, then we want her to get better with us by her side. Nothing is more important than that.

But then, out of nowhere—or, perhaps, catapulted from the most selfish recesses of my brain—the thought comes to me: what if she asks me to break up with Joy now?

For her sake? I push the thought away and focus on Miranda and, because this is my forte, on what needs to be done. On the next step.

"When are you seeing the doctor again?" I'll happily clear my schedule to go with her if she lets me.

"Tuesday," she whimpers. "Biopsy."

"Okay." She has a number of difficult days ahead, filled with insecurity. "What do you need?"

"I need... I need for this not to be cancer." Miranda isn't the most stoic person I know, but the speed at which she's falling apart doesn't befit her personality either. But she has suffered so much already. Joy and I caused her pain. That's why she's coming undone.

"We're going to put you to bed now, okay?" It's late. She's drunk and over-emotional. The best thing she can do is sleep it off and look at it with fresh eyes—and renewed zeal —tomorrow.

"I'll take her," Joy offers. Her cheeks are streaked with tears. She takes her mother by the arm. "I'll be here in the morning, Mum," she says. "I'll stay the night."

"I'll be right up," Jeff says, and kisses her on the cheek tenderly.

While we wait for the stumbling upstairs to subside and Joy to come down, Jeff and I sit. I feel more exhausted than I've felt in months, suddenly aware of the gravity of the situation. I also scold myself inwardly for even thinking about myself in Miranda's hour of need. Perhaps I've changed into a selfish woman, I ponder, when Jeff asks me if I want a drink.

I'm not sure if I should stay. If this were to have happened before Joy and I got together, I would have surely stayed in the guest room, but now, even that feels wrong. I don't know if Miranda wants me to spend the night in her house.

"Sure, I'll have one. Scotch, please." I'm still wearing my coat and I shrug it off me.

"No ice," Jeff says. "No ice for Alice." I wonder what he's had to endure the past few weeks. If he's really the only person Miranda has told, then, I guess, quite a lot.

"She's going to be all right," he says, with his usual Jeff optimism. "I just know it."

"Look, Jeff," I start. "I'm sorry for everything, for how I've hurt Miranda. I never meant to hurt her." It's my turn to feel tears well up, but I've always been very skilled at keeping them at bay.

He sighs. "Do I think it's an easy situation?" he asks rhetorically. "No, I do not. But, do I think the whole thing has been blown way out of proportion?" He continues his questionnaire with himself. "Oh yes, I do. In her head, Miranda has turned you and Joy's relationship into all sorts of things it's not." He shakes his head and stares into his glass. "And I kept telling her that it's only love, it's not a conspiracy, or a plot against her, but, well, she didn't want to hear it."

While I do feel slightly mortified to be talking about this with Jeff, I'm also touched. "I appreciate you saying that."

"That's not to say I wasn't shocked when she told me." He gives one of his loud chuckles—because Jeff is not the kind of guy who chuckles discreetly. "Honestly, I was here when Miranda called you in Portugal to ask if Joy could come over for a few days, and I believe my exact words to Joy were: 'Enjoy the little time you have at the house, because I'm positive Alice is going to boot you out within the next twenty-four hours.'"

Despite myself, I have to laugh at that. And I'm glad for the comic relief it brings. "God, I wanted to. When she first arrived, I wanted her to be gone so much. She was just too much. The way she carried on, so reckless and not taking my feelings into consideration. But, well, she quickly won me over…" While I'm not sure I should be saying these things to Jeff, the sheer relief of simply talking about Joy with another person without being scolded for it, feels so unabashedly good, I can't stop myself. "But you can trust in the fact that I am most shocked of all about how things turned out. The word 'unexpected' doesn't even begin to cover it." Talking to Jeff makes me realise once more how much I've missed my best friend.

"She's asleep." Joy must have descended the stairs so quietly, we didn't hear her come in. "I gave her a sleeping pill. So she should at least have a good night's kip."

"Are you okay?" Jeff asks. It's obvious Joy is still on the verge of tears.

"I can't lose her as well." There's a crack in her voice.

I push myself out of the sofa and hurry towards her. I take Joy in my arms and don't feel the least bit apprehensive about Jeff witnessing our display of affection.

"You, er, are both welcome to stay," he says.

"That's very nice of you," I reply, while still hugging Joy, my face protruding over her shoulder as I look at him. "But I'm not sure Miranda would be comfortable with that. My house is so close, anyway. I'll be here first thing in the morning."

Joy pushes herself away from me. "I need you here tonight, Alice. Please."

How can I possibly refuse her? It doesn't sit entirely right with me to stay without Miranda's explicit permission, because having us both stay over under her roof is still an entirely different thing to process than us being together in my house or at Joy's flat. Or perhaps it's just like that in my head.

"Mum doesn't even have to know. She'll sleep late. Just, please, stay."

"Okay." I nod. "I guess I can stay in the guest room."

Joy looks at me incredulously. She still has her own room in Miranda's house. But I have to draw the line somewhere, not just for Miranda's sake, but for my own as well.

"Let me get that sorted for you." Jeff finishes his Scotch and gets up. "I'll get you some fresh sheets and towels."

"Thank you." I can see he's keen to leave the room.

As soon as we hear him climb the stairs, Joy says, "There's no way we're sleeping in separate bedrooms. Not tonight."

"Joy, honey, I understand how you feel, but we need to show at least a modicum of respect for your mother's wishes. It just… doesn't feel right."

"I'm not asking you to fuck me, Alice. Just… hold me and be there when I wake up."

"Just put yourself in Miranda's shoes. What if she wakes up in the middle of the night and goes to check on you and finds me in your bed?"

"Alice, you're overthinking this. First of all, there's no way she's going to wake up in the middle of the night after taking that pill. And second, we'll both sleep in the guest room, and she would never check there—nor would she check my room, for that matter. If it makes you feel any better, I'll set my alarm for six, so we're both up and about by the time anyone else wakes up."

This is the first time I can clearly feel the duality of wanting to be there for Miranda as a friend and wanting the same thing for Joy but as her partner. No matter which option I choose, I'll be going against my instincts. I can't win. So, in the end, of course I choose to sleep with Joy. If just to erase that forlorn look on her face—tonight of all nights.

"Okay." I pull her to me again. "I love you," I whisper in her ear when I embrace her, because I do.

✶ ✶ ✶

"I remember when you stayed here after Dad died," Joy says when we're both tucked under the covers. I'm wearing one of Miranda's nightgowns. I was hardly going to crawl into bed with Joy naked. She offered me one of the tank tops she sleeps in, but it just looked too ridiculous. "You did everything for us. You cooked. You made me sandwiches when I knew the school lunch was going to be horrible, which was most of the time."

I must have stayed in this room for three weeks, because I didn't want to leave Miranda alone with all her grief. A few months later, long after I'd gone back to my own house, I suggested she sell the house and start making memories in a new place—unfettered by the memory of all the years she'd spent in that house with Paul—but she wouldn't have any of that. Instead, not even six months later, Jeff moved in. The way Miranda rushed into that, clearly driven by grief, I never thought it would last.

"You were so fussy. You brought home a piece of paper with the school menu, showed it to me, and said, 'I don't like that, and that, and that.'"

"You're a good person, Alice, that's all I'm trying to say." She scoots a little closer. "I've always remembered that about you."

"It's what friends do."

"You miss Mum too, don't you?" she whispers, as though it's too hard a question to say out loud.

"I do," I confess, trying to not convey with my tone of voice exactly how much.

"I'm so scared, Alice." Joy's voice grows even softer. "I'd give anything to not have to go through that again."

"I know, sweetheart, I know." I cradle her more snugly in the crook of my shoulder. "But no matter what happens, you won't be alone. I'm here." In the back of my mind, I can't help but wonder, though, what or who exactly she'd give up for Miranda not to have cancer.

✶ ✶ ✶

The next morning, Joy's alarm rouses us at six o'clock. With all the night activity that's been crammed into my schedule, my sleeping pattern has changed of late and I'm still tired when I open my eyes. Joy, however, seems wide awake.

"Did you get some sleep?" I ask.

"No, not really," she says. "Every time I started drifting off and let my mind go, I could only think of one thing: Mum coming down the stairs after Dad died. The look on her face. She didn't even have to say anything, because I knew. I somehow felt it. And even though we knew it was inevitable, and it could happen at any time, it was still so devastating. And nothing at all could console me. Not even the thought that at least now he wouldn't be in pain anymore. It was just so utterly awful."

"I know, honey, I know."

"I guess that's when I decided that I was just going to enjoy my life and not care what anyone thought of me, you know? In memory of Dad. It felt like something I had to do for him. It was also very much how he lived. You know what kind of a loud-mouthed bordering-on-arrogant man he was. He just didn't care. When he died, all I wanted was to become more like him. I think I succeeded."

"You are a brave, honest, good-hearted woman, Joy. I know Paul would be so immensely proud of you."

"What would he think of us, though? What if he were still alive, Alice? What would he have to say about us sharing a bed in his house?"

Good question. Paul has been dead for so long, it seems like a waste of time to even consider his possible opinion. But it's a good moral-compass thinking exercise. "You knew him best," I say, because I really have no clue what he would have thought of me being with Joy this way.

"It's hard to say, of course, because it's been so long now, and I only remember the best parts of him. And, at his best, I'm not saying he wouldn't have minded, but I don't think he would have objected to it the way Mum has. I bet she wished she could have had my other parent present for this, to ask him for advice on how to handle it all. I like to believe that he would have put his hands on my shoulders the way he used to do, and said, "Joy Perkins, you go out and live your life and don't compromise."

"I can see him saying that." It's true. *Don't compromise* was Paul's go-to phrase. Then, a stumbling noise in the hallway makes us jump.

"Oh, shit." Joy seems frazzled as well. "I'll go see if it's Mum or Jeff." Joy slips from underneath the covers and, chastely, puts on the robe that is hanging from the back of the bedroom door.

When the door shuts behind her, I lie back, listening with one ear to the noise beyond the wall, and thinking about what a strange weekend it has already been—and it has only just started. Then, all I can think of is how much I hope Miranda will be okay. This family is so close to unravelling already, another cancer case will be the end of it —literally and figuratively. If the lump is malignant and Miranda doesn't pull through, Joy won't have any parents left alive anymore. That's just not right for someone who hasn't even turned thirty yet. Not that losing your parents is easy at any age—my own mother died of a stroke when she was sixty-eight, my father not long after, at the age of seventy-five, of a heart attack.

"I'm genetically predisposed for cardiovascular disease," I used to say to Miranda when she was on my case about my rigid workout schedule—which I've severely neglected since falling in love with Joy—and my healthy salads for lunch. "If I don't do this, I may not make it past retirement."

"Keep working the way you do, and you won't make it past sixty," she said, which I always shrugged off because work always energised me more than it stressed me, but I see now that she had a point. Life is too fragile to just let it pass you by. I only have to think about the woman at the other end of the hallway to hammer that point home to myself.

"It was just Jeff. He's making breakfast in bed for Mum." Joy drops the robe on the floor and clambers back into bed with me. "She's still out like a light apparently."

"I'm glad I didn't let you go," I say out of the blue. "I'm glad I didn't let anything stand in our way."

"I'm glad, too," Joy says, while she slips her body half over mine. "And I love you, too."

CHAPTER TWENTY-FOUR

On Tuesday, I'm the one accompanying Miranda to her biopsy. Jeff offered to go with her, but Miranda wanted only me to come.

"It's a girl thing," she told him, but I guess she wanted to spare him in a way. Being the spouse of a seriously ill person is no walk in the park, a fact Miranda is more than well aware of. "Besides, Alice and I need to catch up."

By then, we have had more personal conversations in one weekend than in the two previous months combined, culminating in a legendary statement from Miranda saying, "If this is benign and I don't have cancer, you can even call me your mother-in-law, Alice. I will be so over the moon, and will have put everything in so much perspective, that I won't give a damn anymore." Granted, she uttered these words after a fair number of large G&Ts, but still, I hope to be able to remind her of them in due course.

"Listen," Miranda says now, "at the risk of sounding overly dramatic and like we're starring in an episode of *Casualty*." She grabs hold of my arm in the back of the taxi. "If anything happens to me, I mean, er, if worse comes to worst, promise me you won't let Joy fall apart. Promise me you'll be there for her, Alice, no matter what. I need to know that. I need you to promise me that." There's a hitch in her voice and she looks out of the window, unable to face me.

"Nothing of the sort will happen to you." I put a hand on hers, and I can feel that she's trembling. She's scared and nervous. So am I.

"You don't know that. When Paul first went into

hospital, they gave him an eighty percent chance of survival and he's been dead for fourteen years."

"I know, but at this stage… we don't know anything yet, really."

"I know that I'm scared. I'm scared of my daughter having to lose me now after she's already had to lose her father so young."

I can tell this is important to her, so I decide to humour her—even though all this talk is much too defeatist. "Whether it's malignant or not, you will beat this, Miranda," I say. "But, I promise you that, in the very unlikely case of anything happening to you, I will take care of Joy." I hesitate. "I love her. I will do anything I can for her." Did I go too far? Should I not have said that in front of Miranda, who is still looking out of the window?

"I know you love her. Why else would you go through the torment of being with your best friend's daughter? In the end, that has been the most consoling fact—perhaps the very thing that pushed me over the edge once I could think about it with a clear head. I know you so very well, and, in spite of accusing you of being menopausal and delusional, I know that you wouldn't have chosen to be with her if you didn't really, unequivocally, care for her and… love her."

"I know it's hard," I whisper, wondering what the cabbie must think, but then remembering Joy's words from Saturday morning: *I decided not to care anymore what anyone else thinks of me.* "It's been hard on me too."

Miranda inhales deeply and from the corner of my eye, I see her turning towards me. "You make her happy. She's a different person now, although I assume the current circumstances have something to do with that as well. But I've never seen her this relaxed. So at ease with herself. Not since she came back from the States, where, let's face it, she only fled to because she couldn't bear Jeff living in our house and she wanted to punish me."

"If it's any consolation, I still fail to grasp exactly what happened to me. Every single morning, I think to myself, is this really happening? But it is, and, what can I say? I've never been so happy either."

"I know. That's what aggravated me the most about seeing you at the office. I was sitting there fuming while I could actually see the physical change in you. God, it only made it worse to think that my daughter had that effect on you. You're not the same Alice as the one who left for Portugal. I should never even have suggested you take a break from work and insisted you go on holiday." She gives a heartfelt giggle. "I basically pushed her into your arms."

"I should have disagreed with you more strongly when you called," I reply.

"I knew you wouldn't protest too much, Alice. You're simply too good-natured."

"Well, it is *your* house. What was I going to say?"

Miranda grins. "I also know you would never have made the slightest move to seduce Joy, not even if you were suddenly experiencing feelings for her. I know full well how she prances about the villa, without a care in the world or a shred of clothing on her body. Believe me, Alice, I insisted she not do that while you were in the house with her. I explicitly told her how uncomfortable that would make you feel. But Joy doesn't listen to me when it comes to certain matters. Well, most matters, actually. Maybe I was too lax with her after Paul died, I don't know. All I know is that when that girl sets her mind to something, she usually gets it. Be it a college education in California or my best friend as her... her lover."

The taxi stops. We've arrived at the hospital. It's go-time. I go through the registration process with Miranda, but I can't go into the treatment room with her. I take a seat in the waiting area, and wait, all the while thinking that if this is our happy ending, it's a really dubious one.

★ ★ ★

I've taken the entire day off to spend with Miranda. On the

way back to her house, she's quiet. It will take a week until we get the results and it's going to be a long, agonising one.

"Maybe you should go away," I offer. "Go to Portugal. Start practicing for that early retirement you're so keen on."

"God, Alice. I said some godawful things to you. I *am* sorry. I hope you know that."

"There's really no need to apologise."

"There is. Last Friday, after I returned from that disastrous doctor's appointment and the extra, unexpected tests I was subjected to, I went home and sat staring at my phone. I didn't want to call Joy, because I didn't want to alarm her unnecessarily. I was only going to tell her after I'd had the needle biopsy and if the outcome was bad because I didn't want to scare her for nothing. I really, really wanted to call you, but then the spiral of gloomy thoughts started up again in my head. It was Friday late afternoon. You'd be on your way out, quite possibly to see Joy, and I got so angry again. Not because you were seeing Joy per se, but because you weren't at my disposal.

"You're *my* friend, Alice. You have been for decades. And I needed you so badly in that moment, because nobody else would do. Not Jeff with his relentless optimism, nor any of my other friends, because they're not you. They haven't seen me at my worst the way you have. I knew that I could only accept the words 'it's going to be all right' from your lips in that dreadful moment, and you weren't available to me. That's why I hit the sherry. Then I got so drunk not even Jeff could keep me from calling Joy. I shouldn't have done that. I shouldn't have done so many things. But hell, I was hardly thinking about the big picture. The only thing I could think of was how you had abandoned me for my daughter and, when I saw you at work, I wanted to scream, 'What about me, Alice? What about all the time we used to spend together? What about *my* feelings?'" She grabs my hand again. I can hear her sniffing away some tears. "So, I *am* truly sorry for the way I treated you. Who am I to blame you for falling in love with someone as wonderful as Joy?"

"If it makes you feel any better, I will gladly accept your apology, but I'm hardly innocent in this matter. I could have said no. I could have put you first, because I knew how hard this would be for you."

"But why would you do that? When, as long as I have known you, you *have* always put me first. You've held up the business while I was busy raising my child, when I lost my husband, and when I started working less. You have always been there for me, and the one time you needed my understanding, I turned into a monster."

"I think you're being a bit too hard on yourself," I say. "Neither one of us expected you to embrace our relationship. It's a bit too complex for that."

"True, but I could have been easier on you; I could have been a tad more forgiving. Even Jeff asked me at a certain point whether I was willing to go as far as losing you both over it, while all you and Joy had done wrong in my eyes was fall in love." She rummages in her purse for a tissue. When she doesn't find one, I hand her one from the full packet I always carry with me. "The things I said to him after that." She shakes her head while wiping her nose. "It wasn't pretty."

"It's all perfectly understandable," I say, while rejoicing on the inside because, by the sound of it, I have my best friend back. I can only hope, with everything I have, that I get to keep her for a very long time to come.

"Tell me it's going to be all right, Alice. I need to hear it from you again."

"Miranda Jones. This time next week we'll be having a massive party with bottle after bottle of champagne because we'll be celebrating the good outcome of your biopsy. You're my best friend and my life is not the same without you, so I simply refuse to lose you."

"Thank you." She leans her head on my shoulder the way Joy does sometimes. And I notice how I've become much more comfortable with tactile displays of friendship. "Say, Alice, I have been meaning to ask you... now that you're, er, a lesbian. Have you, uh, ever been attracted to me?"

I guffaw at her question, then try to reply in a steady voice, "No, Miranda. It's not like—"

"I'm just pulling your leg, Alice." She slaps my thigh.

"For Christ's sake." I bump her away from me with my shoulder.

After she stops snickering, because this is obviously very funny to Miranda, I say, "I never had the chance to tell you, but I ran into Alan a few weeks ago."

"You did?" She turns to me fully.

"Yes. It was a really random encounter." I don't share with Miranda the reason for my long walk that day. "I just ran into him when I walked into a pub I'd never set foot in before. We sat down for a drink, but as soon as I sat across from him, I was appalled at the thought of spending any time at all with him. Not because I still hate him for leaving me for Sheryl. I got over that a long time ago. But because of what he stood for: everything I don't want in a significant other. My life could have been so different if we hadn't divorced, and it was as though I could see it flash before my eyes."

"Did he look that bad?" Miranda jokes.

"No, not even. He looked like a perfectly acceptable middle-aged man. A man who takes proper care of himself and who's comfortable enough in his skin."

"So..." Miranda begins. "Are you... a lesbian now?"

"I don't know." I actually truly don't. "If the singular definition of a lesbian woman is as simple as a woman who has fallen in love with another woman, then I guess I am." I shrug. "I'm not too worried about defining myself, though. I am much more worried about keeping you as my friend."

"I will always be your friend, Alice. We're like a couple in a very long relationship. We can basically finish each other's sentences, but"—another pause—"maybe we will need some rules. You can talk to me about almost everything, of course, but when it concerns Joy, there will be certain things I don't want to hear."

"I didn't have a total personality transplant. I'm not in the habit of pouring out my heart to you. I will always be who I am in that regard."

"You can tell me all the things she refuses to, however, like what time she makes it home on the weekend, and if she's doing any recreational drugs." Miranda looks at me expectantly, then bursts into a smile. "I'm just kidding." She chews her bottom lip for an instant. "All jokes aside. You have changed. You have less of a stick up your arse, if I may be so bold as to use such language."

"Only today," I reply. "Today you can say anything you want to me."

"What do you mean *only* today? I could very well have cancer next week, Alice. At least give me until then."

"You don't have cancer," I say, my voice sounding much more convinced than I ever, realistically, could be. "Who's going to give me hell if you do?"

Seconds later, the taxi pulls up to the curb of Miranda's house. When we go inside, both Jeff and Joy are there. Jeff had taken the day off work, but Joy had told me that, having only just started at her new job, she wasn't able to take a day off yet.

"Surprise," she says. "I made your favourite cake, Mum." The house smells delicious.

"Come here, darling." Miranda tugs Joy towards her. "I still don't think you should have seduced poor, defenceless Alice, but you're the best daughter a mother could ask for."

CHAPTER TWENTY-FIVE

"So, Alice," Joy says the next Saturday afternoon. Jeff has taken Miranda on an impromptu trip to the Cotswolds to take her mind off the impending biopsy result. They're due back on Sunday evening, which gives Joy and me some time for just the two of us.

"Yes." I look up from the book I'm reading. It's the Lee Child book I never got to finish in Portugal.

"Remember, before all hell broke loose last weekend, I told you I had something for you."

"Oh, yes, that's right." I had totally forgotten about that. "What do you have for me, Joy?"

She sits there with a massive twinkle in her eyes. I have absolutely no idea what she could have got me, or what the occasion would be to give me a present.

"Well, I brought it with me. Let me just go and get it from my bag." She rises. "Actually, I think you should come upstairs with me. I think it's better if I show you in the bedroom."

A tingle sprouts in my stomach. What is she up to? "Okay." I put down my book and look at her. She's leaning against the chimney now, and the sparkle in her eyes has possibly got even bigger.

"Come on." She turns on her heel and dashes up the stairs.

Brimming with curiosity, and somehow knowing it's going to be a gift that will make me blush, I follow her. By the time I make it to the bedroom, she's sitting on the bed with a wrapped rectangular box in her hands.

"You know I love you, Alice. I'm actually completely besotted with you. And, I guess, now that Mum has given us her blessing, I would like to take things to the next level."

A quick wave of panic hits me. Is this one of those lesbian things I read about on the internet? About moving in after the second date, and proposing marriage after only a few months together? That doesn't fit with the box she's holding, though, nor does it gel, I think, with Joy's personality. "Yes…" I say, hesitantly.

"Well, here you go." She hands me the package. Perhaps she wrapped the keys to her flat in an elaborate wooden box, although we've been spending more and more time at my house, because it's closer to her mother, and, without any pomp or circumstance, I handed her a key to my front door a few days ago.

I take the wrapped box from her and shake it about a bit. It's very light. Then, curiosity gets the best of me, and I start tearing the paper off while trying to remember when someone gave me a present last. It was probably Miranda for my birthday last year. When all the wrapping paper has come off, I see a plastic box with, inside on full display, a… penis-shaped object in all the colours of the rainbow. I can't help but stare at it in silence for long seconds. I'm not looking at Joy at all, but it's as though I can sense her sitting there very pleased with herself for some reason.

"Do you know what that is?" she asks, her voice all sugary and sweet.

"I th-think I have an idea," I stammer. I haven't lived that sheltered a life to not recognise this particular object when I see it in my own hands, but never had I thought that this was the present Joy was going to give me.

"How do you feel about my gift?" Joy slides a bit further onto the bed, slips her legs under her bottom, and regards me as though she's interviewing me for *Newsnight*.

How *do* I feel about it? A little apprehensive, I guess. A tad insecure. And, come to think of it, incredibly aroused.

"Why does it have these colours?" I ask.

"No reason," Joy says. "I just liked them best." She slants her head to the side. "Do you want to take it out of the box? Take a closer look?" Joy's voice is growing lower in pitch. I can almost see the excitement grow in her glance. This is turning her on greatly.

"Sure." I sit down next to her and fumble with the box until I hold its contents in my hands. This is a dildo, I think, and it's not a thought I've ever had in my life, and it doesn't fail to instantly connect with that pulsing beat between my legs. Inside the box, there's a soft black pouch, and, uncontrollably impatient as she seems, Joy takes it out, opens it and shows me what's inside.

"It comes with this." She holds an intricately intertwined black ribbon in her hands. "These are the straps," she says.

"I see," I say. Straps for what? I want to ask, but don't want to come across as completely ignorant.

"It's a strap-on harness," Joy says, her voice almost liquid. "You put the dildo in like this." She picks up the rainbow-coloured contraption and holds it in front of the hole in the larger, padded piece of fabric to which the ribbons are attached. "And I really, really, really would like to fuck you with it."

"Would you now?" I ask. My own voice seems to have dropped an octave as well. I can't hide my arousal at seeing Joy with her hands all over this toy she has bought, and—despite my initial confusion—especially at what she just said.

"Oh, yes," Joy says, but must have somehow picked up on my trepidation, or my hesitation when she explained to me how it works. "It doesn't have to be now. Whenever you feel ready." Our eyes meet, and she may very well want to display patience with her words, but in her glance I see none.

Do I want this? Of course, I'm staring into Joy's lust-filled eyes, and when I do, I want everything she wants—and possibly even more. And I want to know what it feels like.

Joy has clearly done this before, otherwise she wouldn't appear so utterly excited about it.

"I might be ready now," I say, because oh, how my blood is beating in my veins and how my heart is racing.

"Yeah?" She sinks her teeth into her bottom lip and inches towards me. So close, I can feel her body heat radiate onto me, I can smell my brand of soap on her. And Joy so close to me is always intoxicating.

"Oh, yes," I reply, and kiss her. Instantly, she pulls me to her and while, when we usually kiss, we gradually move into a more frantic, more urgent rhythm, this kiss is intense from the very beginning, like a clear declaration of intent. Maybe this is taking it to the next level then.

"You drive me crazy, Alice," Joy says, when we break from our lip-lock. "You know why?"

"No," I say, while I grab for her neck again.

Her lips are by my ear when she speaks next. "Because you're such a proper lady outside the bedroom, but inside, you're up for anything. That drives me so, so wild."

"Only for you," I whisper, not even sure she can hear me. But it doesn't matter, because Joy has started to push me down onto the bed, and I willingly let her. She kisses my lips, then my neck, then lets her lips travel down the opening of my blouse until she can't go any further.

"Let's get these off," she says, and when she looks at me I see all her love for me blazing in her eyes, and it makes me slip right into the divine state of abandon—that state where one moment I'm dressed and the next, as though I myself had nothing to do with it, I'm naked, and ready for Joy to do whatever she wants with me.

I push myself up and get my clothes off as quickly as I can, because my own patience has run out as well. We've had such an emotionally demanding week, with barely any time for each other, and though it's been cathartic in a way to have Miranda back in our lives, it has also been stressful to wait for the test results. I want my mind to go empty. I crave that blank space where thoughts cease and I'm just my body. A body Joy knows how to manipulate expertly.

"Let me see if I still know how to do this," Joy says, and scoots off the bed. She grabs the toy and the harness, inserts one into the other, until an almost obscene image of her emerges, although the silly rainbow colours do take away from that a bit. She steps into the contraption and starts fastening the straps around her hips and behind. She does it so confidently, without any display of nerves whatsoever— the way she always is in bed with me, coaxing me through the highest high as though it's her only expertise in life— that, by the time she's fully strapped-on my blood is beating so hotly in my veins, I need her back in bed with me pronto.

But she stands there for an instant, a defiant glint in her eyes, as if she wants to say, 'Look how far I got you, Alice. Look how incredibly aroused I have made you. You'd better be ready for this because I'm going to give you the time of your life.' It's such a typical Joy stance. It's basically how she seduced me. That youthful, unbridled confidence she has won me right over with.

"Come here," I whisper, because I have a voice too, and I've learned how to express my needs with it.

She sits on the bed almost reverently, as if this is a big moment for us. Maybe it is. It will certainly be a new experience for me. The dildo protrudes from between her legs and, because of the colours, it could be a comical display. It's anything but.

"I love you," Joy says, and bows down to kiss me, and I consider these three simple words. How they have changed my life. How they can have so much meaning although, according to what Joy has told me, in the US they've become more of a catchphrase than an expression of deep feelings. One of the reasons she had to get out of there, she claimed. And it's all these little facts she fills my day-to-day life with that have changed everything for me on such a grand scale. Like a ripple effect, her coming into my life, with this huge giant bang of orgasm after orgasm in Portugal, followed by all the introspection we had to subject ourselves to because of who we are and the relationships we have, and all the tidbits she has shared. How she brought me outside myself, and broke the shell I was living my comfortable but, truth be told, emotionless life in. It's all the little things and the big things that have made us who we are today, here in my bedroom, a late afternoon autumn sun slanting through the window. But what's about to happen now, I would definitely catalogue under the big things.

"I love you, too," I say. A simple truth. A life-changing statement. A sentiment that's about to come to its full, most glorious expression.

Joy manoeuvres herself on top of me, and I feel the dildo press against my thigh, and to have this other thing, this object not part of our bodies, but strangely part of hers anyway, in bed with us is exhilarating, because of what it promises. Another new sensation. I've had so many the past few months. And I'm really proud of myself for taking everything in my stride so quickly—not easily, but with consideration and courage.

She fondles my breast with her right hand, while she kisses me again and I can feel her love for me every time our lips touch. Because Joy has changed, too. At first, I couldn't possibly fathom what a girl like Joy would want with middle-aged, repressed me. But she has shown me what and who I am to her. And she has gradually revealed the real me to myself. This is she, I think. This is me. A woman about to be fucked by her lesbian lover with a strap-on dildo. When I think back to the woman who boarded that plane to Portugal at the beginning of August, she and I could not be further removed from each other, in spirit as well as everything else.

Joy's hand meanders down, and I know what she will find, and I also know what's she's going to say, because she's the kind of person who likes to say things out loud—a fact that never fails to turn me on even more.

"God, you're so wet, Alice." I smile, because there's arousal in familiarity, too. Oh God, there is. I want Joy over and over again, until she's taken all of me and, even then, if she were to ask me, I would still spread my legs for her. Because when we're like this, in this bubble of supreme intimacy, there's nothing I wouldn't do for her—for us.

Before I know it, Joy's finger has slipped inside me, and she keeps kissing me, and the dildo keeps pressing against my thigh, and I can't wait for her to enter me with it. A desire I didn't even know I possessed grabs hold of me, and makes me react swifter to the thrusting motion of her fingers—two now—and makes me groan into her mouth as her tongue swirls inside mine.

"Fuck me, Joy," I say for the first time ever. "Fuck me with the dildo." It's a word I'd never thought I'd say, and it intensifies the heat in my blood, the throbbing between my legs, the way my wet, wet sex wraps itself around her fingers.

She smiles down at me. The best thing about Joy, who is someone who likes to talk about every little thing, is that she does also know when to shut up. Now is one of these moments. Because no words are needed now. This might be a new experience, but it's one so inherently natural, so of all times and of all people, that we can just go with the flow we've created.

Joy pushes herself away from me for an instant and repositions herself between my legs. She looks at me down there and flicks her tongue over her lips. She's like a predator, like she's the cougar about to devour her prey. She scuttles closer, presses my legs farther apart, until I feel the dildo make contact. It's a shocking sensation, but not as shocking as when she starts rubbing the head along my lips, her fingers trailing behind it. She avoids my clitoris, wisely, just drags the tip of the toy along my lips, up and down, until she rests it at my entrance. She rubs her palm along its length, spreading my juices over it, and the sight of that makes me gasp for air again—and I was already so out of breath.

Then, she shifts her hips, and starts to slide in, ever so slowly. It's an entirely new feeling to have this foreign object slipped into me. It's wide, and filling, and long. Inside me, it feels so much bigger than when I looked at it. I feel stretched, inhabited, taken, and it's the best feeling in the world. Joy has moved her upper body so it's supported by her arms, which are planted just above my shoulders. She looks into my eyes as she, gradually, increases the speed of her motion.

She's fucking me, I think. She's actually doing this. *I'm* actually doing this. And isn't that the strangest thing of all? Me, lying here, on my very own bed, the one I've slept in for decades, with another woman on top of me who is fucking me like this?

But I don't have any inclination to think further than that, because I've reached that particular headspace again, the one where it's just the most exquisite white noise occupying my brain, where all thoughts cease, where nothing is more important than what is happening to my body right now. And a lot is happening as Joy's thrusts arouse me more and more. I get carried away by the intensity of the moans coming from my own throat, and Joy's narrowed eyes on me, and the slight grunting sound she makes every time she pushes into me, and how the girth of the dildo stretches me wider than I've ever felt, and how it touches a spot inside me.

"Argh," I moan, still slightly unaccustomed to the sound of my own voice when it goes high-pitched and loose like that.

"Ooh," Joy groans in response, and it's as though we're working in tandem to give me the utmost pleasure, although she's really doing all the work. She increases the motion of her hips, makes it faster still, and I wrap my legs around her behind, tether her to me, as though I never want to let go again. I don't.

Then, the delicious crash is inevitable. She has taken me to a new high, a plane so out of this world, I see everything in a new, golden light. I feel my blood beat, I feel my skin zing with excitement, I feel the drop of sweat sliding down my temple, I feel the thrust of the dildo inside every cell of my body. I'm purely a physical being, freed of all emotion that may possibly harm me or depress me or stress me. I'm just *me* in my purest form, until I start plummeting down from that high, and Joy catches me. She always does.

"Oh my God," I holler. "Oh. Oh. Ooh." The orgasm that takes me is so strong, so obliterating, my eyes fill with tears.

Joy slows her strokes and looks at me with a sweet smile on her face, as though she can't quite believe it herself. It happened, I want to say, but the lump in the back of my throat is so big, no words can get past.

Instead of speaking, I pull her to me and shower her in kisses, while she slowly lets the dildo slip from me. *You're everything*, I want to say, *everything I've ever wanted and so much more*. But I don't even have to say it, because she knows. After what she has just done to me, she surely knows.

CHAPTER TWENTY-SIX

"Screw the job," Joy says, when I ask her if she's sure she can take the time off. "I want to be there for Mum when she gets the news." We're at the Jones & McAllister office, where she has come to pick up Miranda to take her to her doctor's appointment, the one where she'll get the results. "And let's be honest here, Alice. If they decide to fire me, I could easily be a kept woman." She lets her gaze sweep over my office. "You've basically worked enough hours in your life to cover my career." She pins her gaze on me again.

"And here I was thinking *you*'d be supporting *me* in my old age." I lean back in my chair. It's strange to have her here, in my office. To mix this very personal thing with business. Although, I guess, it has always been very intertwined, what with Miranda and I being friends first and business partners second.

"You know I'm only with you for your body and your exquisite mind, Alice. Not for your money. But, come to think of it, nursing home fees are so steep these days. I think I will tell Mum I no longer agree with her early retirement plan."

Last night, over dinner at Miranda's, we danced around the subject of a positive or negative outcome as best we could, but Miranda did express a renewed interest in retiring sooner rather than later—perhaps in a year or two. Not because she can't bear to face me in the office every day, but because she wants to travel more, enjoy life more, and not have the burden of running a business and all the stress it causes. I could hardly disagree, because I, too, have felt a subtle shift.

Work is no longer the first thing on my mind when I wake in the morning and stare into Joy's face. The next day's to-do list no longer occupies any space in my brain before I close my eyes, because Joy is there to erase the slightest inkling of it. Over lunch, I often venture out, even if I don't have an appointment I need to get to, just to be outside and get swallowed into the humdrum of the city and, quite simply, forget about work for half an hour. Not only has my personal life changed, my perspective on work has shifted as well.

"Maybe Miranda and I should both retire." I can hardly believe the words coming from my mouth, but Joy is right. At only fifty-one, I *have* worked enough hours to fill the course of two full-time careers, and for what? As much as I enjoy my work, I find pleasure in many other activities now, and maybe it's time to start enjoying those more.

"Hold your horses, Alice." Joy regards me with an amused look on her face. "Whatever would you do with yourself all day while I'm grafting hard targeting Facebook and Twitter ads?"

"I don't know. Perhaps try to wrap my head around what exactly it is you do at work." Joy has tried to explain it to me many times, but I don't seem to have a brain willing to grasp her core business. "And cook you dinner. Do your laundry. Bring you lunch. Just be a relaxed housewife."

"Trust me. You'd turn into one of those women who start on the Cabernet at eleven in the morning for lack of something else to do. You're a doer. A worker. You need the stimulation."

"Maybe we'll take on a new partner and I'll work part-time then."

A knock on the door stops our conversation, which, perhaps, isn't finished, or perhaps it is. Maybe my work is too much a part of me to let go just like that.

"Who's going to work part-time?" Miranda asks. Her

posture is rigid, her features tense.

"No one just yet," I reply. "How are you feeling?"

"Rather stressed," Miranda says.

"Come on, Mum." Joy curls an arm around Miranda's shoulder. "We'll make an afternoon of it after we've had the good news. A mani-pedi and all that."

"Call me as soon as you know," I instruct them both and then, completely uncharacteristically, leap from my chair to give Miranda a hug.

"We will," Joy says solemnly, before they both saunter off and I'm left waiting again, not knowing what to do with myself. Within the next hours, all our lives could dramatically change. If Miranda has cancer, voluntary retirement won't even be an option anymore. Our lives will change into what they were when Paul got sick. A perpetual circle of dashed hope, followed by picking ourselves up again, because what other choice will we have?

"No," I tell myself. "Stop it." Even if Miranda's lump turns out to be cancerous, it doesn't mean that it will kill her. But despite the excellent breast cancer survival rates these days, it's just harder to imagine it won't, when you've seen it happen before.

I try to focus on work, but my gaze is glued to my phone screen, while I simultaneously want it to ring and dread the moment it will.

★ ★ ★

Almost two hours after Miranda and Joy left the office, I've driven myself near-mad with reasons why it would take so long to deliver a simple result. Finally, my phone rings and it's Miranda.

"Hello," I say with a trembling voice.

"Alice," Miranda's voice is as high-pitched as I've ever heard. "Oh, Alice," she says, almost gasping, "it's not cancer. It's a fibroadenoma and it's benign."

"Oh, thank Christ," I whisper into the phone. "I'm so happy for you, Miranda."

"We're going out to celebrate. You don't have meetings this afternoon, do you? Come and join us, please. Jeff is coming as well."

"It will be my utmost pleasure." A tension that's been building in my muscles for days finally releases, and, again totally against my character, I feel tears well up.

Miranda tells me where to meet them, after which I quickly hang up and head to the ladies' room.

I dab my tears away and hope no one will come in, while I stare at myself in the mirror. "This is your time," I tell my reflection. "Don't waste your life on things that don't matter any longer." I nod at myself—agreeing with myself—straighten my spine, and walk out.

★ ★ ★

When I find Joy and Miranda—Jeff hasn't arrived yet—at the Oxo Tower bar sipping champagne, I kiss Joy fully on the lips in front of her mother, and I know that I no longer have to care about what Miranda might think.

I hug Miranda for a long time, sit down, sip from the glass she's poured me and look at the pair of them. My best friend and my partner. The two people I love most in the world. And I can't think of a place I'd rather be right now than here.

"I love you both," I say, and raise my glass. "And, Miranda, I hope you remember that promise you made last week."

Miranda looks at me over the rim of her glass. "That you get to call me mother-in-law?" she asks. "Over my dead body, Alice. And I plan to live for a very long time."

I find Joy's gaze and the look she gives me warms me to the core.

ACKNOWLEDGEMENTS

This is a book I've been meaning to write for a long time and I need to thank my family-in-law for introducing me to the Algarve, which turned out to be the perfect setting for Alice's awakening. Thanks also to Maria and Fletcher for taking us around in the area and providing inspiration for Alice's day trips. Special mention to my trusted editor Cheyenne Blue for explaining the difference between a barrister and a solicitor, and the stellar work she always does whipping my books into shape. A big shout out to the members of my Launch Team who helped weed out the remaining typos. And, as always, endless gratitude to my readers. You make all my dreams come true.

Thank you.

ABOUT THE AUTHOR

Harper Bliss is the author of the novels *Once in a Lifetime* and *At the Water's Edge*, the *High Rise* series, the *French Kissing* serial and several other lesbian erotica and romance titles. She is the co-founder of Ladylit Publishing, an independent press focusing on lesbian fiction. Harper lives on an outlying island in Hong Kong with her wife and, regrettably, zero pets.

Harper loves hearing from readers and if you'd like to drop her a note you can do so via harperbliss@gmail.com

Website: www.harperbliss.com
Facebook: facebook.com/HarperBliss
YouTube: youtube.com/c/HarperBliss

Printed in Poland
by Amazon Fulfillment
Poland Sp. z o.o., Wrocław